CAT'S CRADLE

Book 1 · The Golden Twine

JO RIOUX

KIDS CAN PRESS

KIDS CAN PRESS ACKNOWLEDGES THE FINANCIAL SUPPORT OF THE GOVERNMENT OF ONTARIO, THROUGH THE ONTARIO MEDIA DEVELOPMENT CORPORATION'S ONTARIO BOOK INITIATIVE; THE ONTARIO ARTS COUNCIL; THE CANADA COUNCIL FOR THE ARTS; AND THE GOVERNMENT OF CANADA, THROUGH THE CBF, FOR OUR PUBLISHING ACTIVITY.

PUBLISHED IN CANADA BY
KIDS CAN PRESS LTD.
25 DOCKSIDE DRIVE
TORONTO, ON M5A 0B5

PUBLISHED IN THE U.S. BY
KIDS CAN PRESS LTD.
2250 MILITARY ROAD
TONAWANDA, NY 14150

WWW.KIDSCANPRESS.COM

EDITED BY KAREN LI
DESIGNED BY RACHEL DI SALLE

THE HARDCOVER EDITION OF THIS BOOK IS SMYTH SEWN CASEBOUND. THE PAPERBACK EDITION OF THIS BOOK IS LIMP SEWN WITH A DRAWN-ON COVER.

MANUFACTURED IN SHEN ZHEN, GUANG DONG, P.R. CHINA, IN 3/2014 BY PRINTPLUS LIMITED

CM 12 0 9 8 7 6 5 4 3 2 1
CM PA 12 0 9 8 7 6 5 4 3 2

LIBRARY AND ARCHIVES CANADA CATALOGUING IN PUBLICATION

RIOUX, JO-ANNE
        THE GOLDEN TWINE / JO RIOUX.

(CAT'S CRADLE)
ISBN 978-1-55453-636-8 (BOUND)   ISBN 978-1-55453-637-5 (PBK.)

I. TITLE. II. SERIES: RIOUX, JO-ANNE. CAT'S CRADLE.

PN6733.R56G65 2012   J741.5'971   C2012-900814-1

Kids Can Press is a l©rus™ Entertainment company

To Keith, for always believing in me.

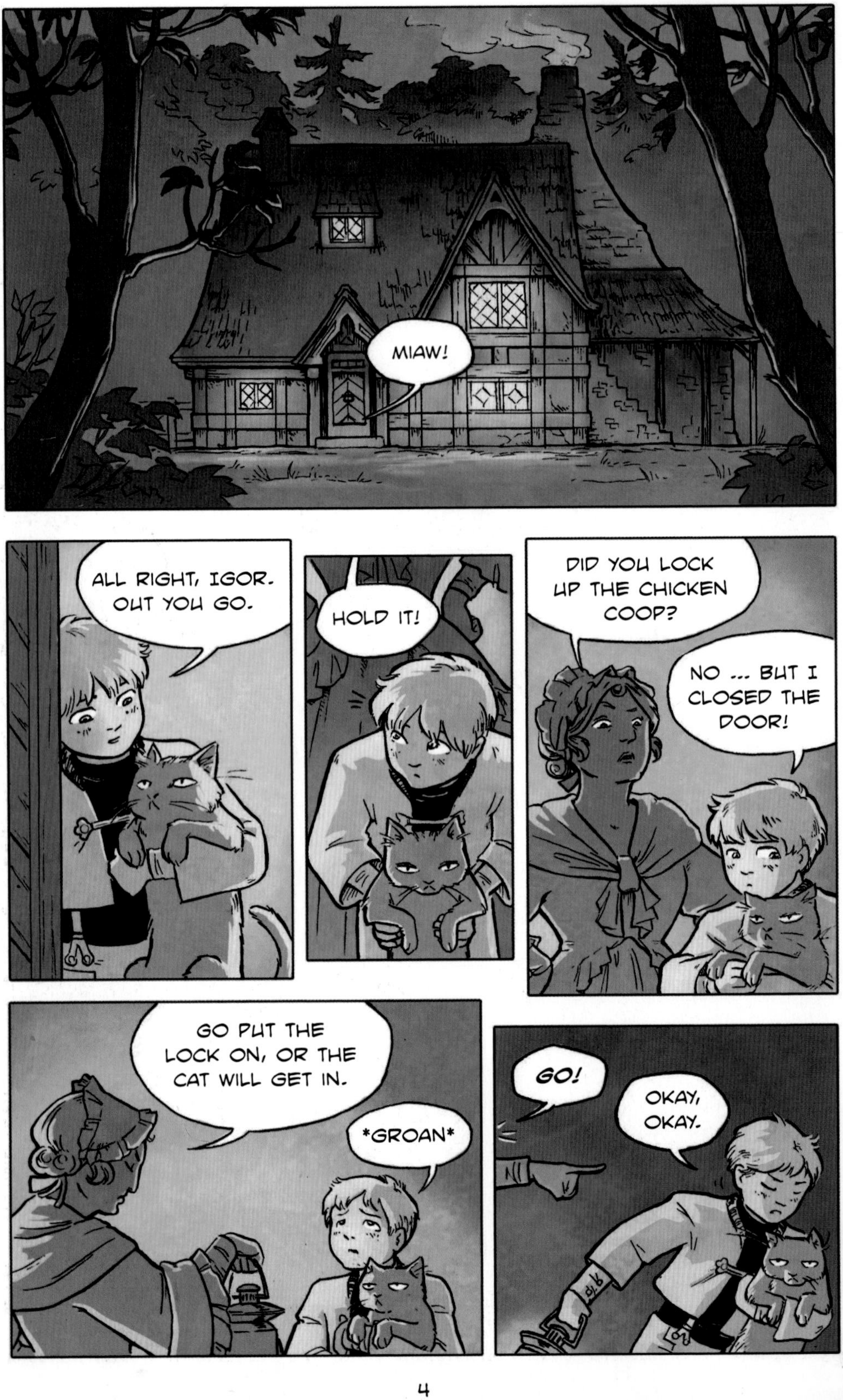
MIAW!
ALL RIGHT, IGOR. OUT YOU GO.
HOLD IT!
DID YOU LOCK UP THE CHICKEN COOP?
NO ... BUT I CLOSED THE DOOR!
GO PUT THE LOCK ON, OR THE CAT WILL GET IN.
GROAN
GO!
OKAY, OKAY.

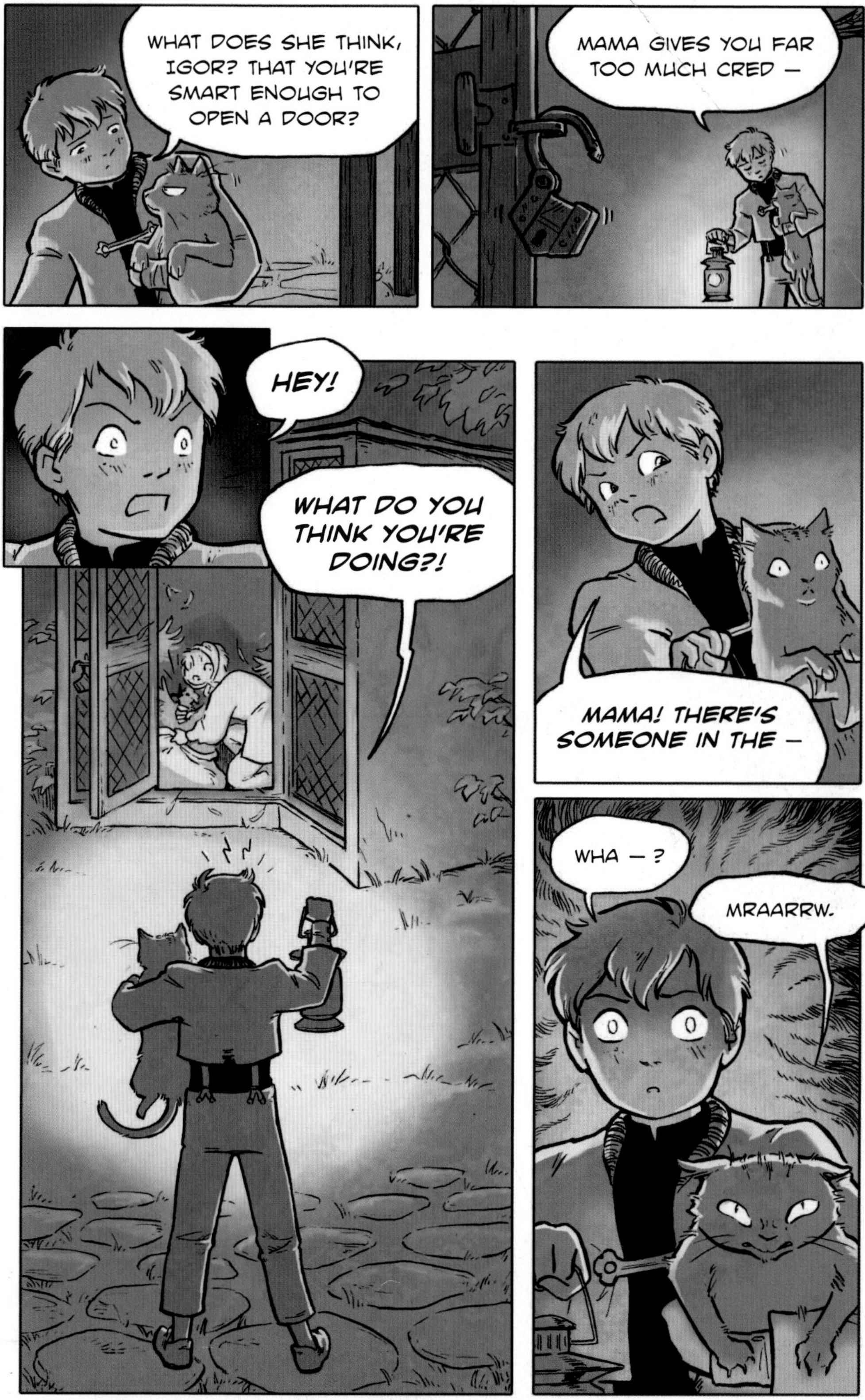
WHAT DOES SHE THINK, IGOR? THAT YOU'RE SMART ENOUGH TO OPEN A DOOR?
MAMA GIVES YOU FAR TOO MUCH CRED —
HEY!
WHAT DO YOU THINK YOU'RE DOING?!
MAMA! THERE'S SOMEONE IN THE —
WHA — ?
MRAARRW.

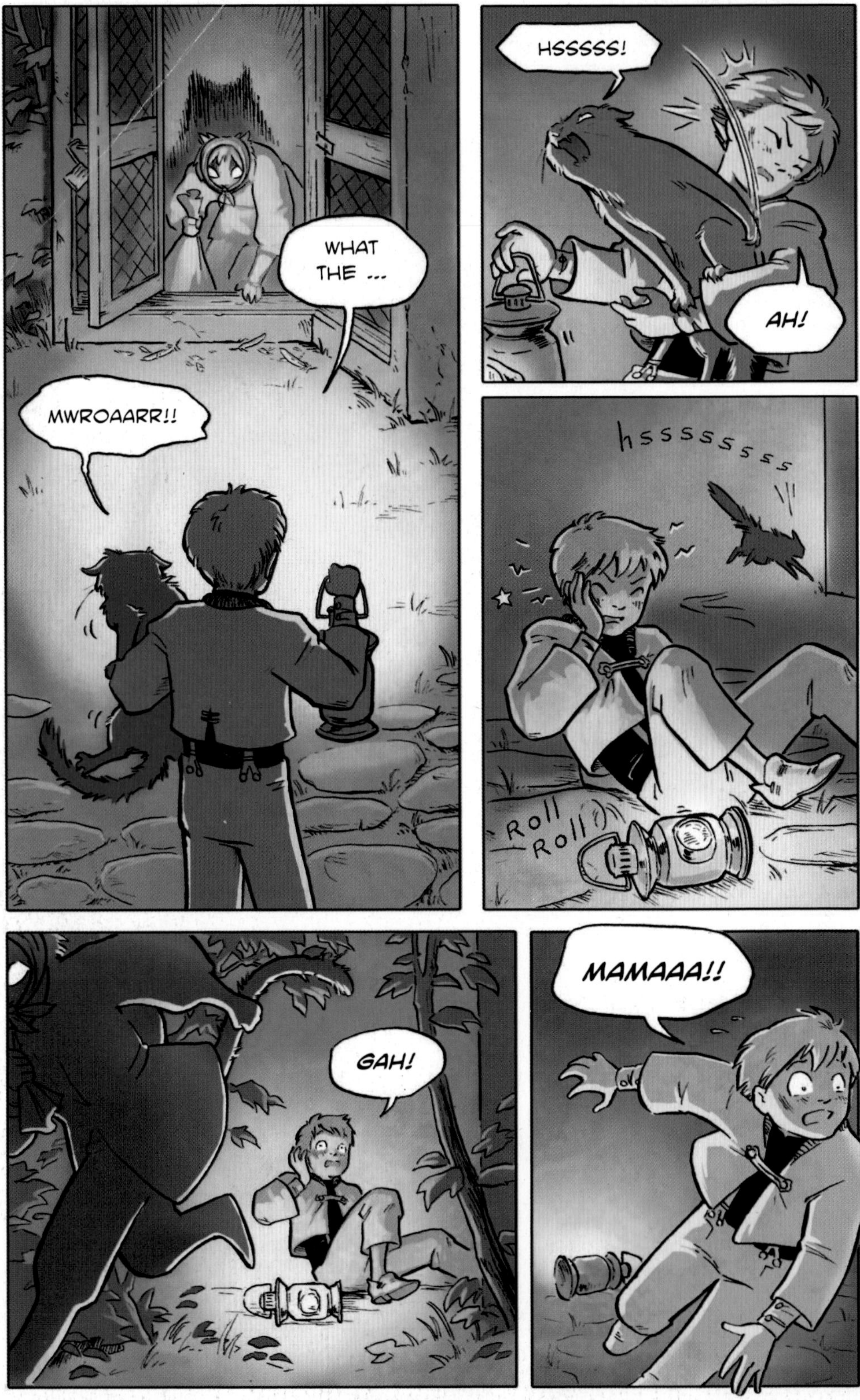

WHAT THE ...
MWROAARR!!
HSSSSS!
AH!
hsssssssss
Roll
Roll
GAH!
MAMAAA!!

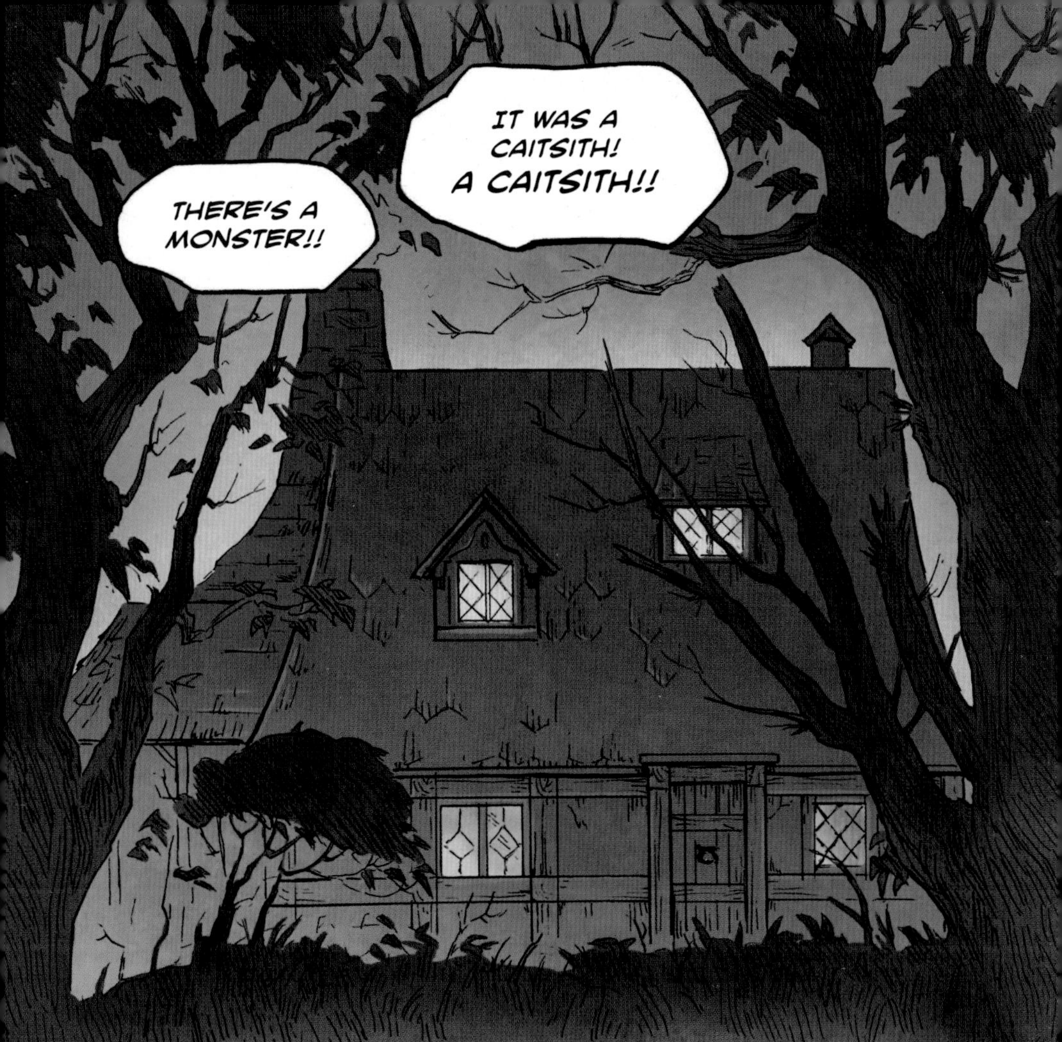
THERE'S A MONSTER!!
IT WAS A CAITSITH! A CAITSITH!!

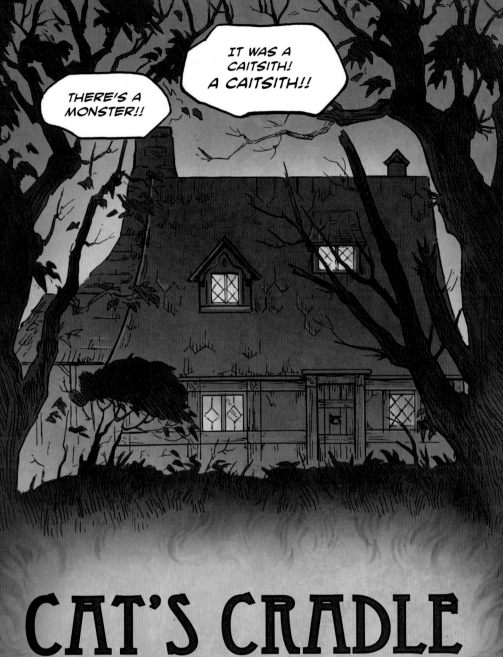

CAT'S CRADLE

Book 1 • The Golden Twine

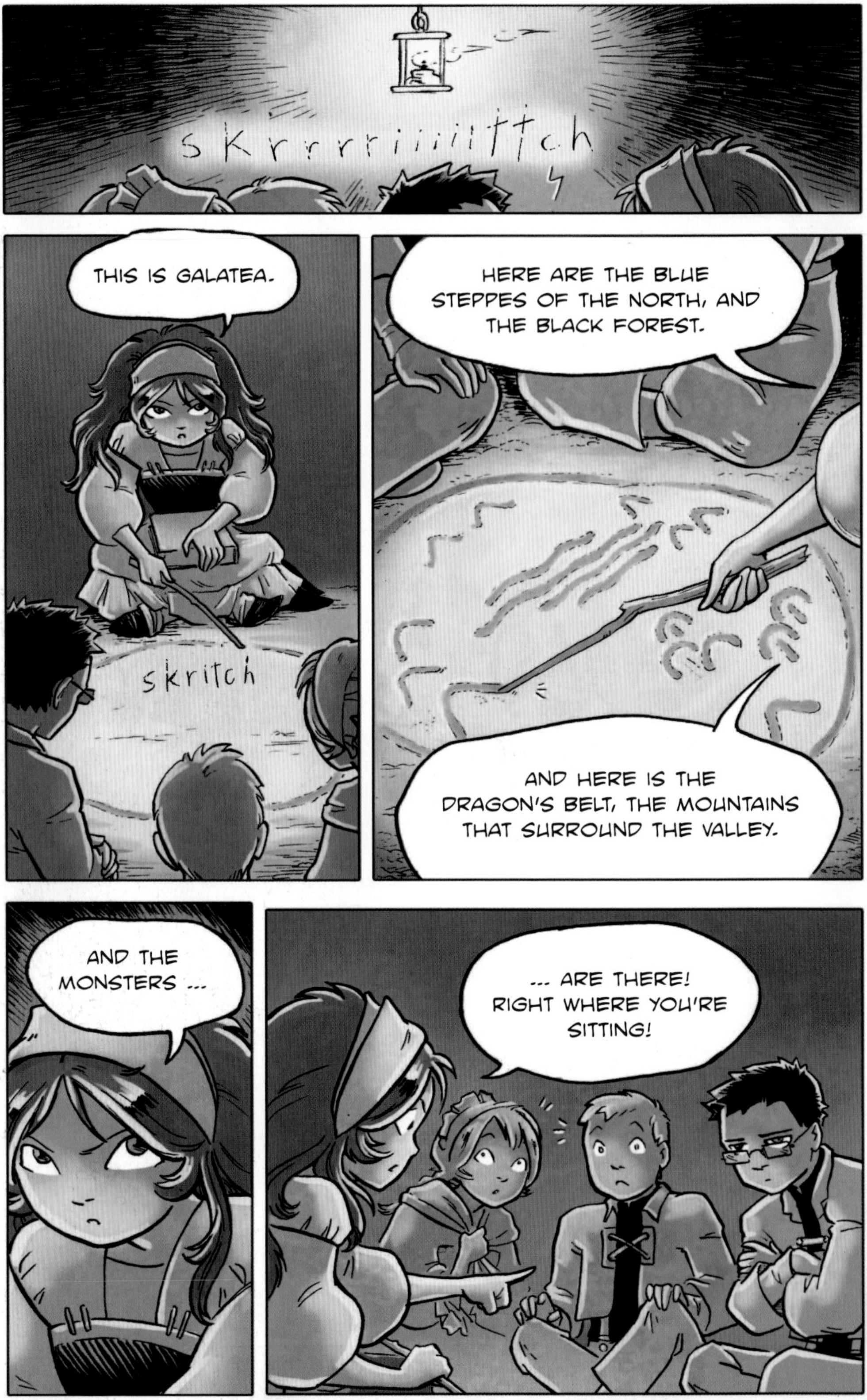
sKrrrriiiiittch
THIS IS GALATEA.
skritch
HERE ARE THE BLUE STEPPES OF THE NORTH, AND THE BLACK FOREST.
AND HERE IS THE DRAGON'S BELT, THE MOUNTAINS THAT SURROUND THE VALLEY.
AND THE MONSTERS ...
... ARE THERE! RIGHT WHERE YOU'RE SITTING!

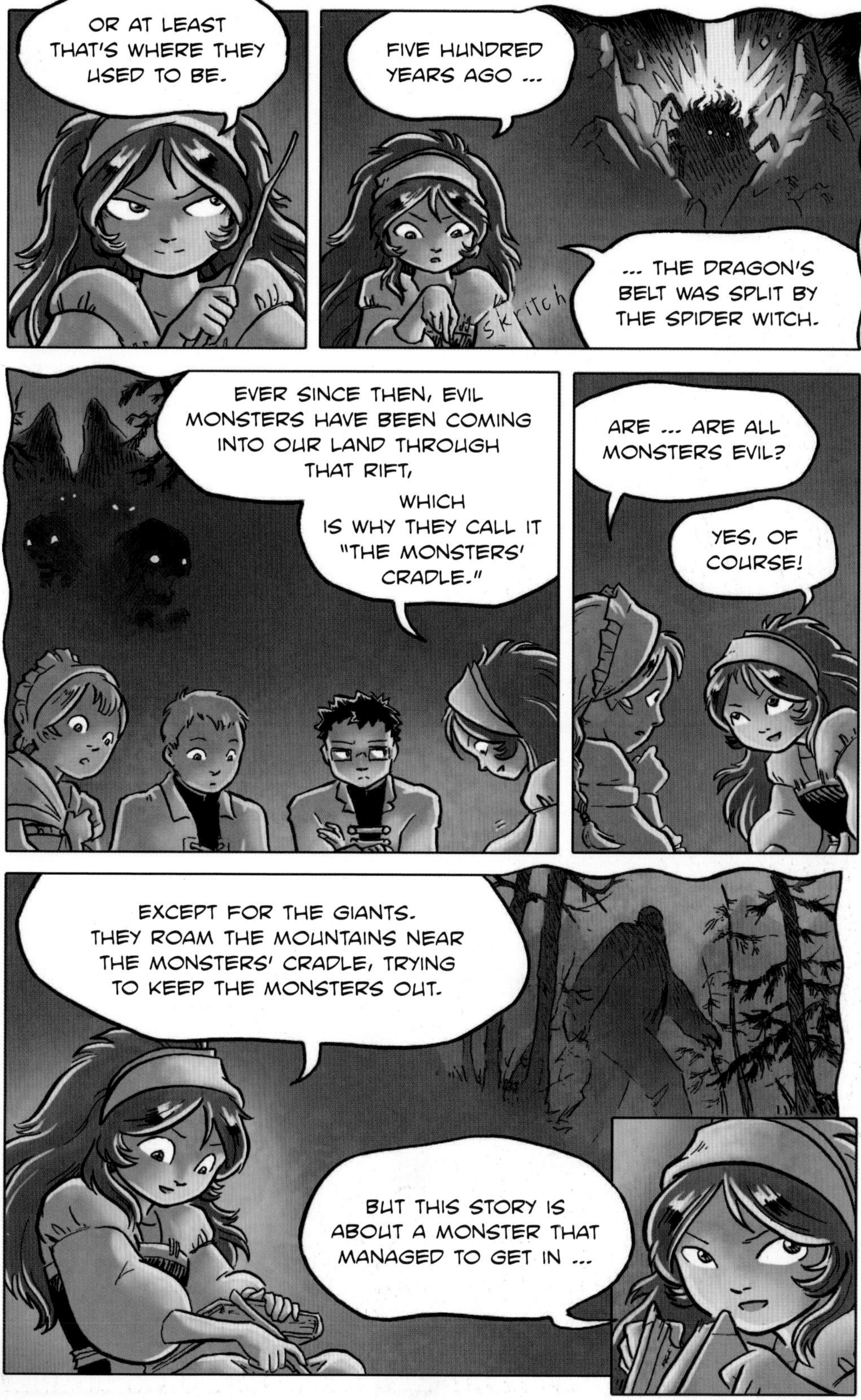
OR AT LEAST THAT'S WHERE THEY USED TO BE.
FIVE HUNDRED YEARS AGO ...
skritch
... THE DRAGON'S BELT WAS SPLIT BY THE SPIDER WITCH.
EVER SINCE THEN, EVIL MONSTERS HAVE BEEN COMING INTO OUR LAND THROUGH THAT RIFT,
WHICH IS WHY THEY CALL IT "THE MONSTERS' CRADLE."
ARE ... ARE ALL MONSTERS EVIL?
YES, OF COURSE!
EXCEPT FOR THE GIANTS. THEY ROAM THE MOUNTAINS NEAR THE MONSTERS' CRADLE, TRYING TO KEEP THE MONSTERS OUT.
BUT THIS STORY IS ABOUT A MONSTER THAT MANAGED TO GET IN ...

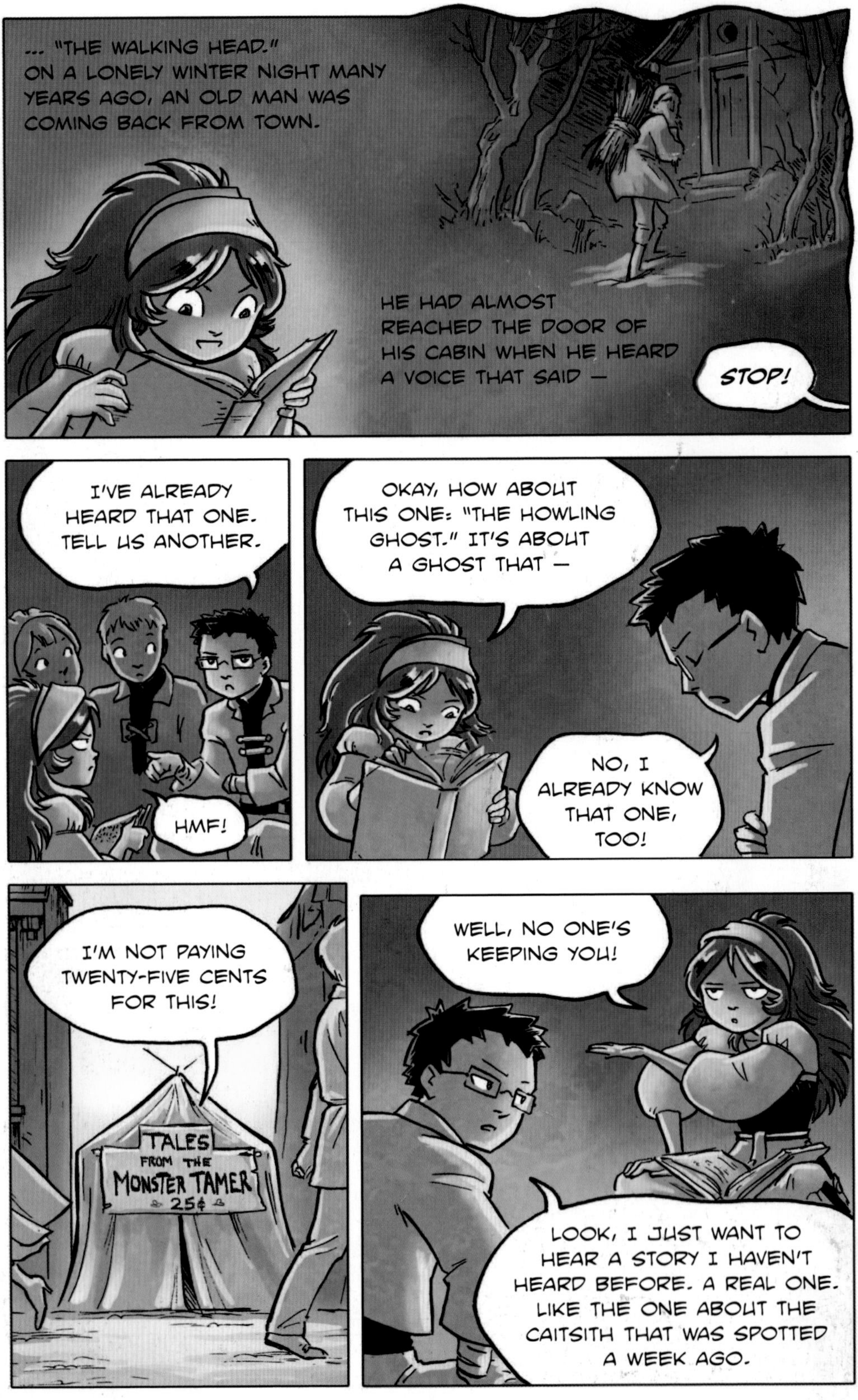
... "THE WALKING HEAD." ON A LONELY WINTER NIGHT MANY YEARS AGO, AN OLD MAN WAS COMING BACK FROM TOWN.
HE HAD ALMOST REACHED THE DOOR OF HIS CABIN WHEN HE HEARD A VOICE THAT SAID —
STOP!
I'VE ALREADY HEARD THAT ONE. TELL US ANOTHER.
HMF!
OKAY, HOW ABOUT THIS ONE: "THE HOWLING GHOST." IT'S ABOUT A GHOST THAT —
NO, I ALREADY KNOW THAT ONE, TOO!
I'M NOT PAYING TWENTY-FIVE CENTS FOR THIS!
TALES FROM THE MONSTER TAMER 25¢
WELL, NO ONE'S KEEPING YOU!
LOOK, I JUST WANT TO HEAR A STORY I HAVEN'T HEARD BEFORE. A REAL ONE. LIKE THE ONE ABOUT THE CAITSITH THAT WAS SPOTTED A WEEK AGO.

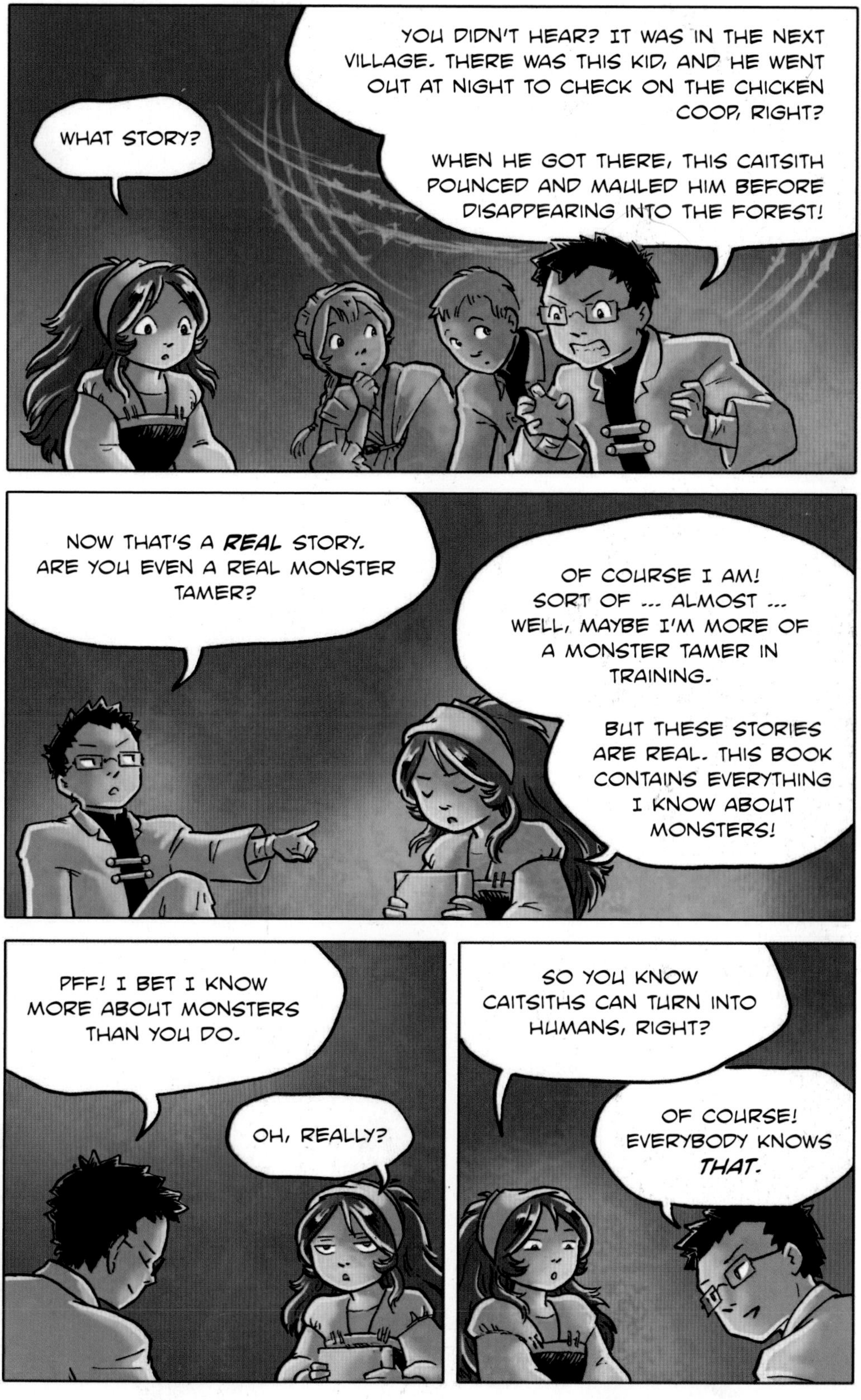
WHAT STORY?
YOU DIDN'T HEAR? IT WAS IN THE NEXT VILLAGE. THERE WAS THIS KID, AND HE WENT OUT AT NIGHT TO CHECK ON THE CHICKEN COOP, RIGHT?
WHEN HE GOT THERE, THIS CAITSITH POUNCED AND MAULED HIM BEFORE DISAPPEARING INTO THE FOREST!
NOW THAT'S A ***REAL*** STORY. ARE YOU EVEN A REAL MONSTER TAMER?
OF COURSE I AM! SORT OF ... ALMOST ... WELL, MAYBE I'M MORE OF A MONSTER TAMER IN TRAINING.
BUT THESE STORIES ARE REAL. THIS BOOK CONTAINS EVERYTHING I KNOW ABOUT MONSTERS!
PFF! I BET I KNOW MORE ABOUT MONSTERS THAN YOU DO.
OH, REALLY?
SO YOU KNOW CAITSITHS CAN TURN INTO HUMANS, RIGHT?
OF COURSE! EVERYBODY KNOWS *THAT*.

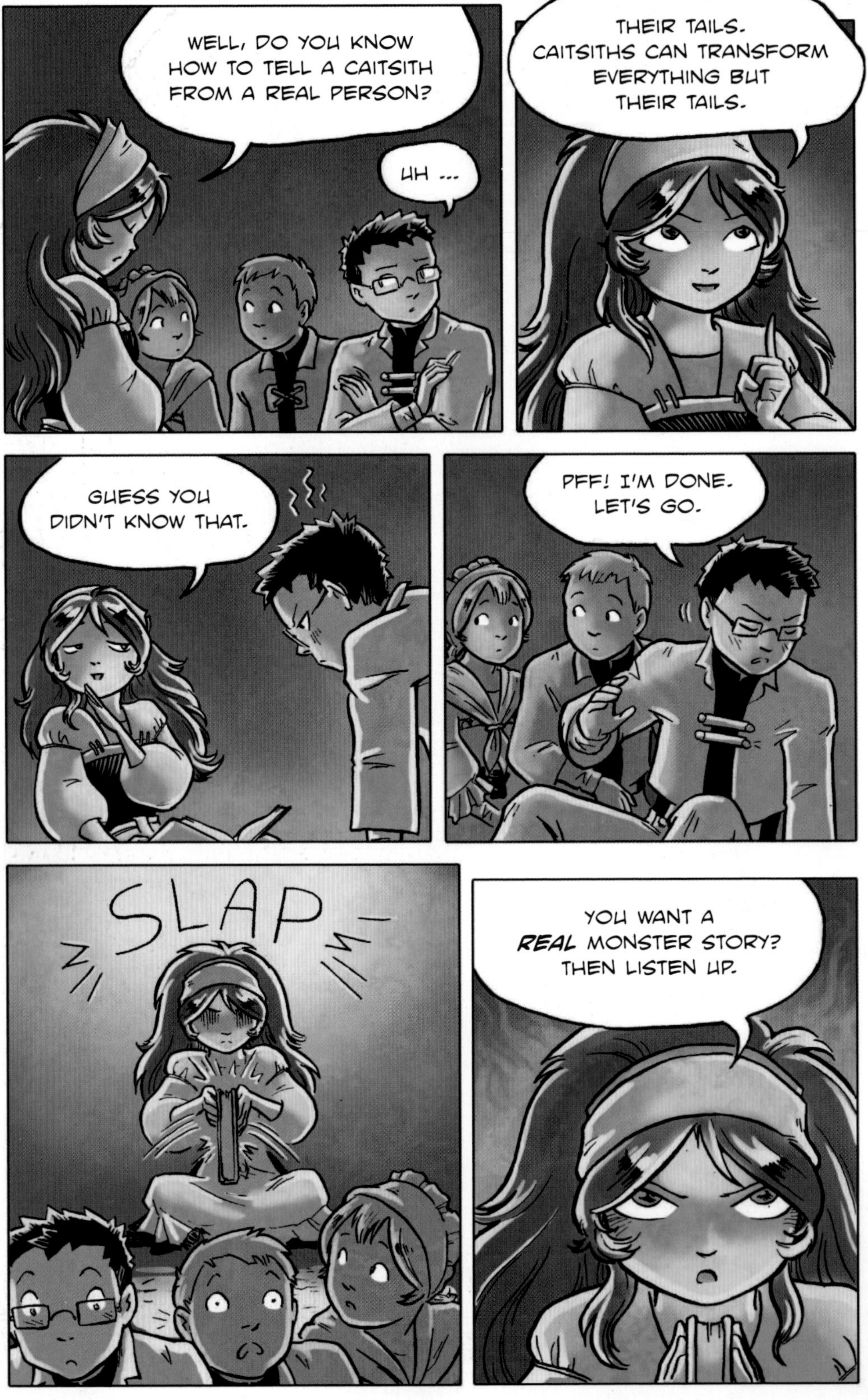
WELL, DO YOU KNOW HOW TO TELL A CAITSITH FROM A REAL PERSON?
UH ...
THEIR TAILS. CAITSITHS CAN TRANSFORM EVERYTHING BUT THEIR TAILS.
GUESS YOU DIDN'T KNOW THAT.
PFF! I'M DONE. LET'S GO.
SLAP
YOU WANT A *REAL* MONSTER STORY? THEN LISTEN UP.

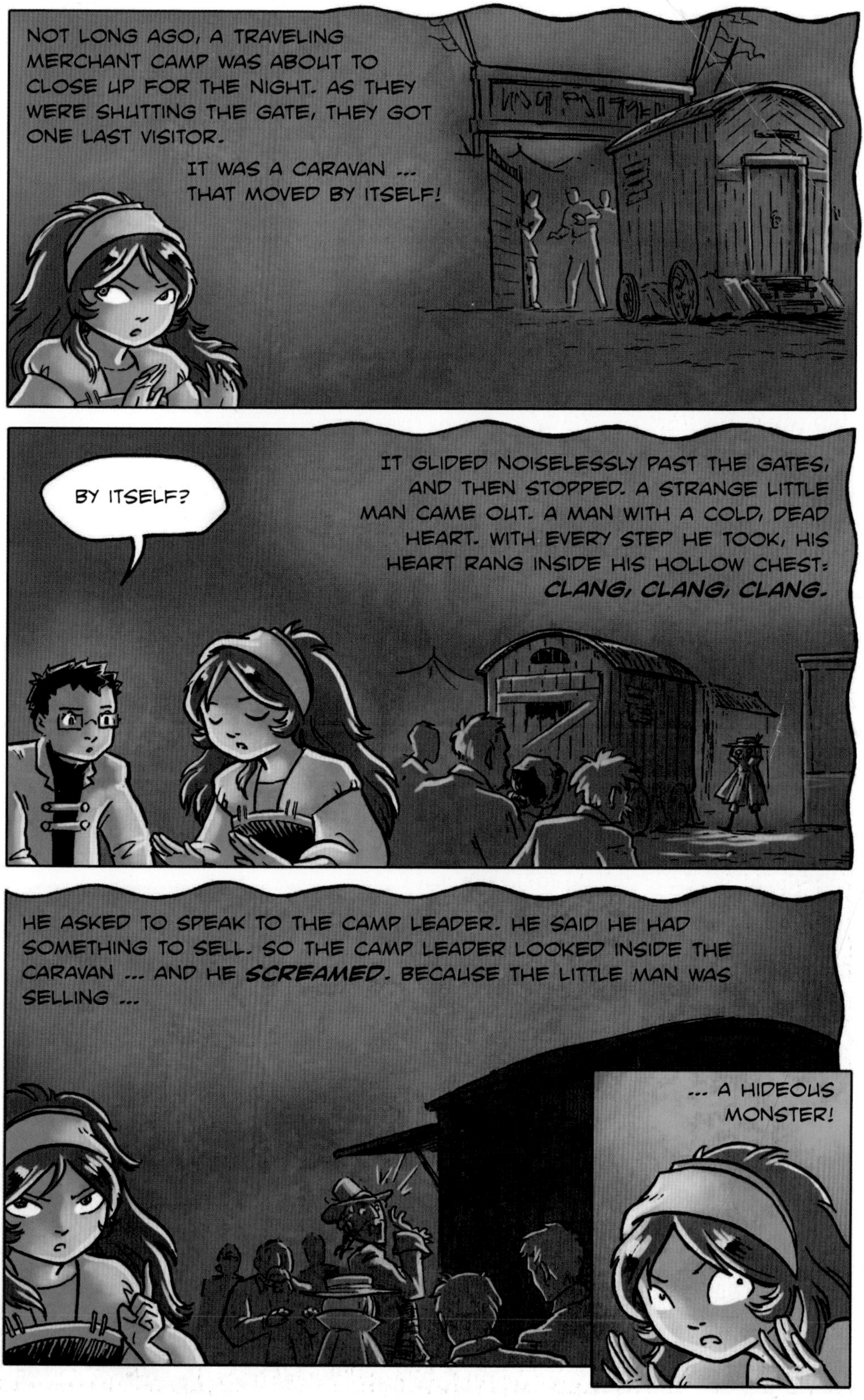
NOT LONG AGO, A TRAVELING MERCHANT CAMP WAS ABOUT TO CLOSE UP FOR THE NIGHT. AS THEY WERE SHUTTING THE GATE, THEY GOT ONE LAST VISITOR.
IT WAS A CARAVAN ... THAT MOVED BY ITSELF!
BY ITSELF?
IT GLIDED NOISELESSLY PAST THE GATES, AND THEN STOPPED. A STRANGE LITTLE MAN CAME OUT. A MAN WITH A COLD, DEAD HEART. WITH EVERY STEP HE TOOK, HIS HEART RANG INSIDE HIS HOLLOW CHEST: ***CLANG, CLANG, CLANG.***
HE ASKED TO SPEAK TO THE CAMP LEADER. HE SAID HE HAD SOMETHING TO SELL. SO THE CAMP LEADER LOOKED INSIDE THE CARAVAN ... AND HE ***SCREAMED.*** BECAUSE THE LITTLE MAN WAS SELLING ...
... A HIDEOUS MONSTER!

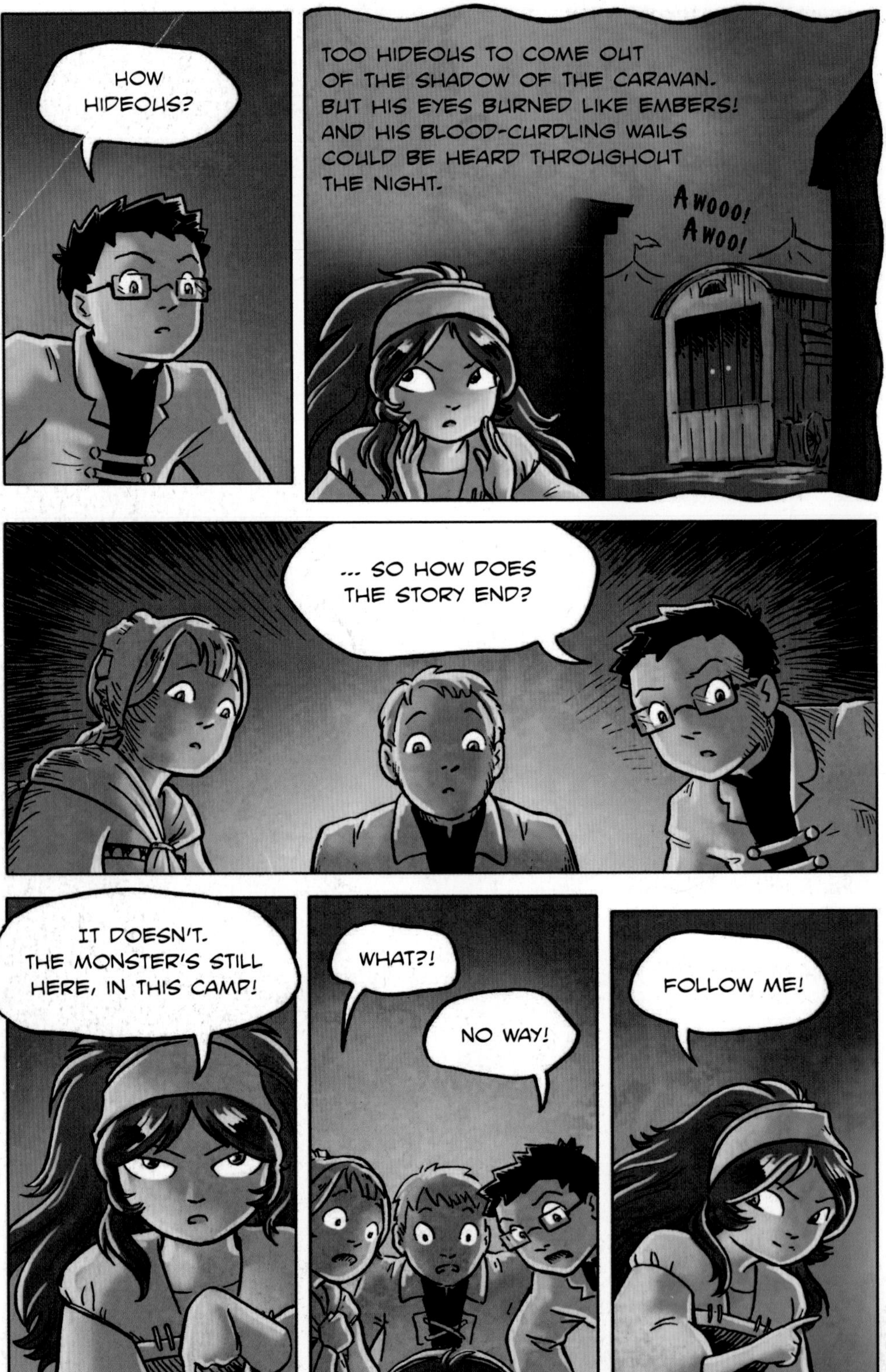
HOW HIDEOUS?
TOO HIDEOUS TO COME OUT OF THE SHADOW OF THE CARAVAN. BUT HIS EYES BURNED LIKE EMBERS! AND HIS BLOOD-CURDLING WAILS COULD BE HEARD THROUGHOUT THE NIGHT.
AWOOO! AWOO!
... SO HOW DOES THE STORY END?
IT DOESN'T. THE MONSTER'S STILL HERE, IN THIS CAMP!
WHAT?!
NO WAY!
FOLLOW ME!

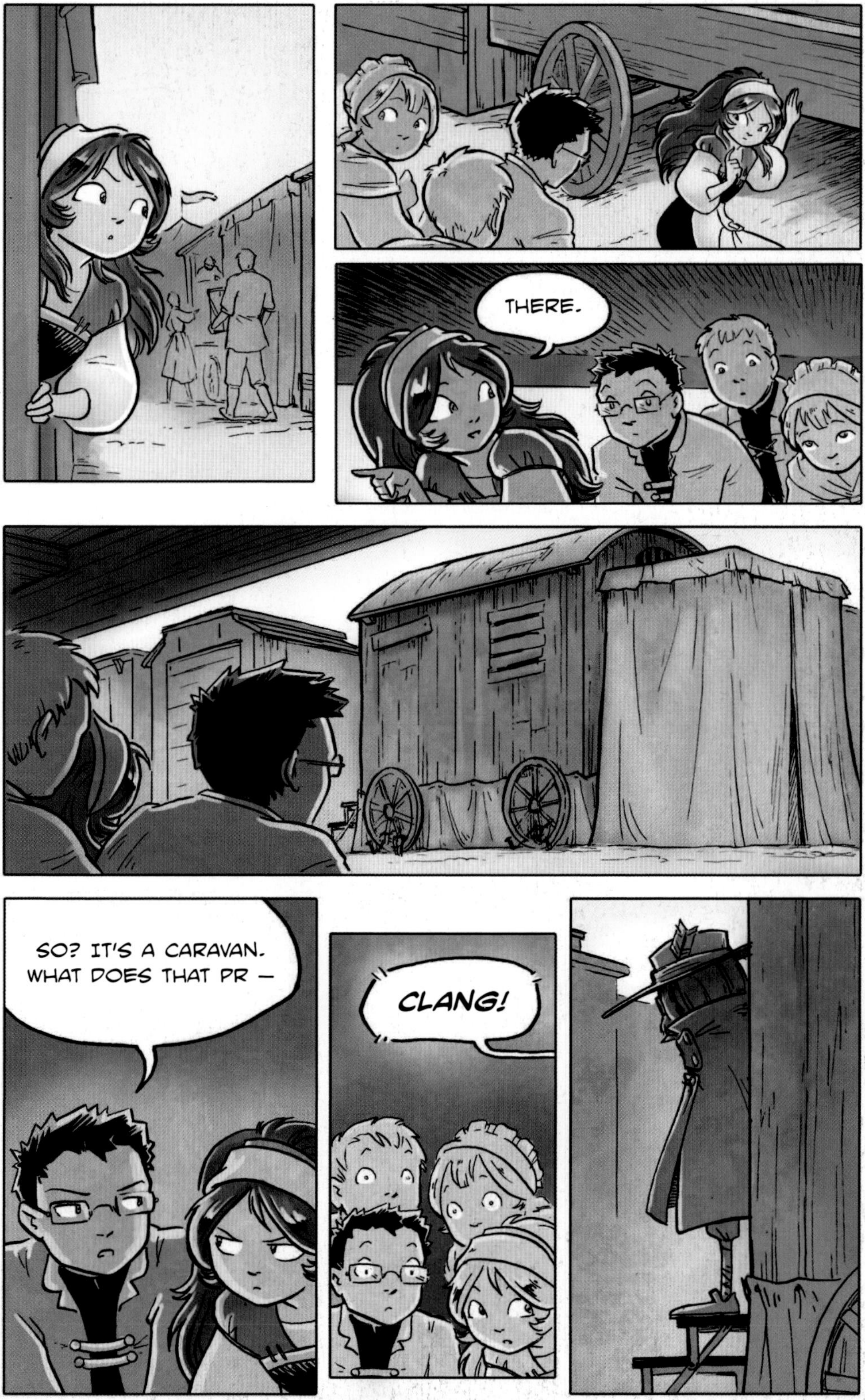
THERE.
SO? IT'S A CARAVAN. WHAT DOES THAT PR —
CLANG!

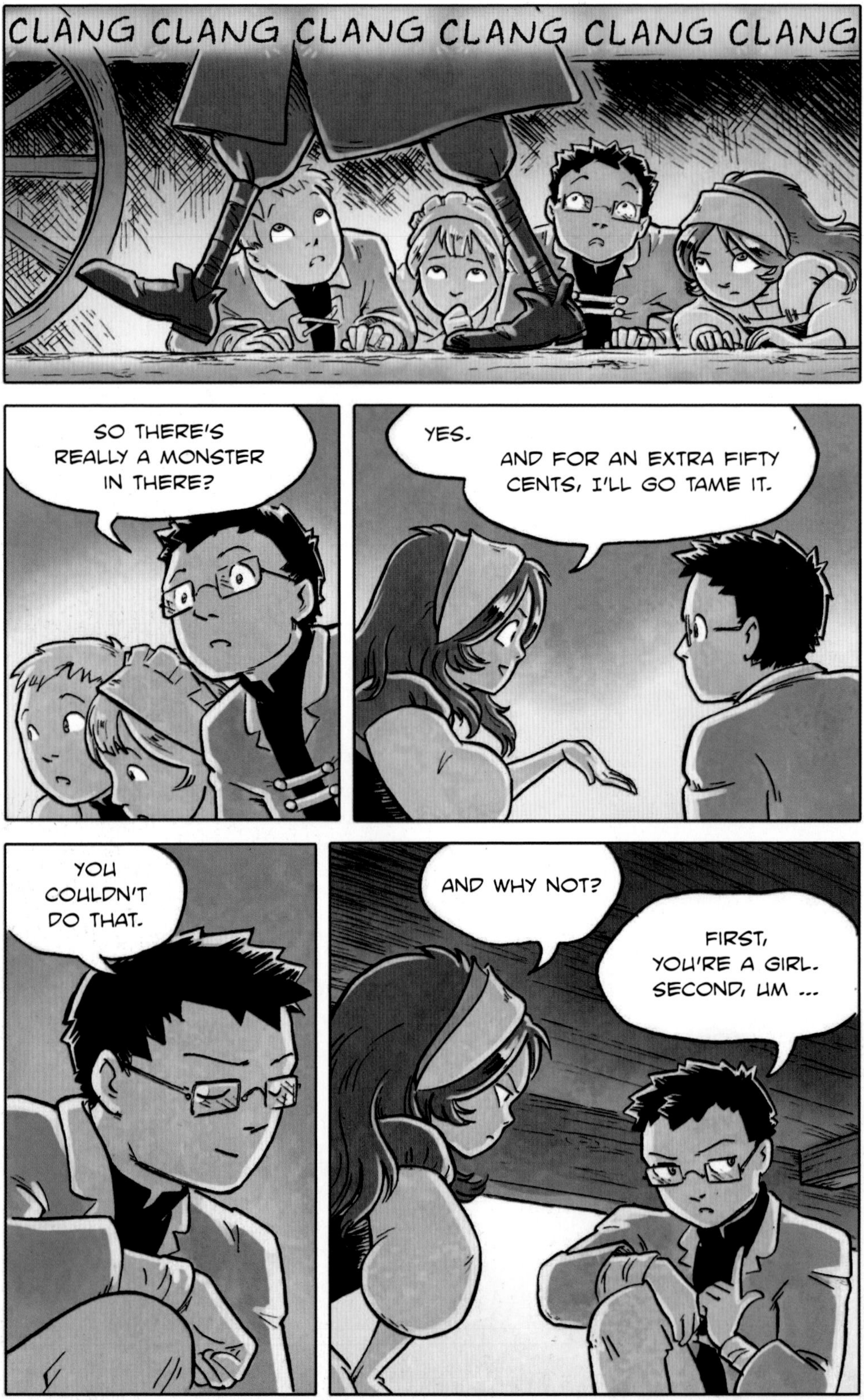
CLANG CLANG CLANG CLANG CLANG CLANG
SO THERE'S REALLY A MONSTER IN THERE?
YES.
AND FOR AN EXTRA FIFTY CENTS, I'LL GO TAME IT.
YOU COULDN'T DO THAT.
AND WHY NOT?
FIRST, YOU'RE A GIRL. SECOND, UM ...

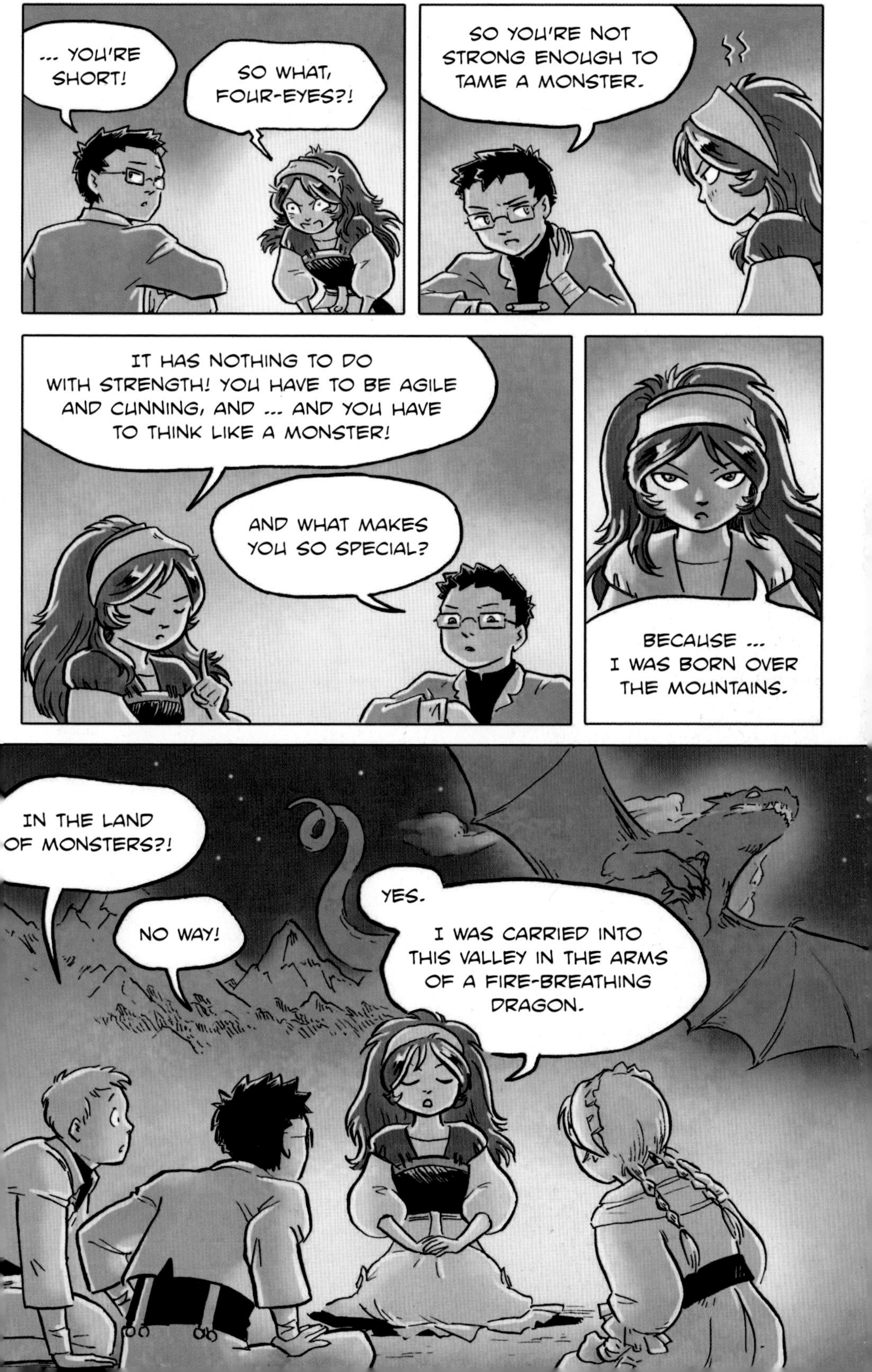
... YOU'RE SHORT!
SO WHAT, FOUR-EYES?!
SO YOU'RE NOT STRONG ENOUGH TO TAME A MONSTER.
IT HAS NOTHING TO DO WITH STRENGTH! YOU HAVE TO BE AGILE AND CUNNING, AND ... AND YOU HAVE TO THINK LIKE A MONSTER!
AND WHAT MAKES YOU SO SPECIAL?
BECAUSE ... I WAS BORN OVER THE MOUNTAINS.
IN THE LAND OF MONSTERS?!
NO WAY!
YES.
I WAS CARRIED INTO THIS VALLEY IN THE ARMS OF A FIRE-BREATHING DRAGON.

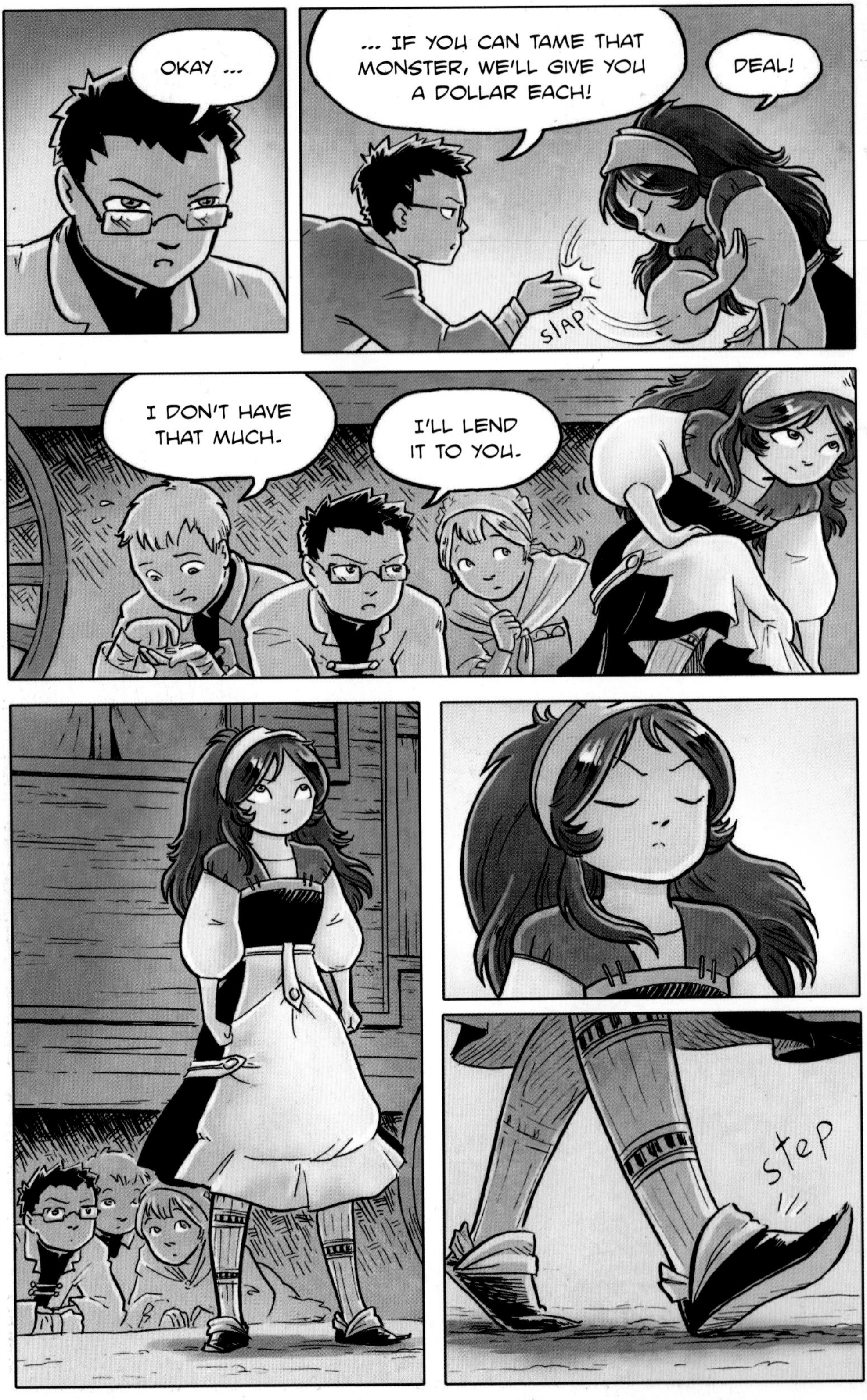
OKAY ...
... IF YOU CAN TAME THAT MONSTER, WE'LL GIVE YOU A DOLLAR EACH!
DEAL!
SLAP
I DON'T HAVE THAT MUCH.
I'LL LEND IT TO YOU.
STEP

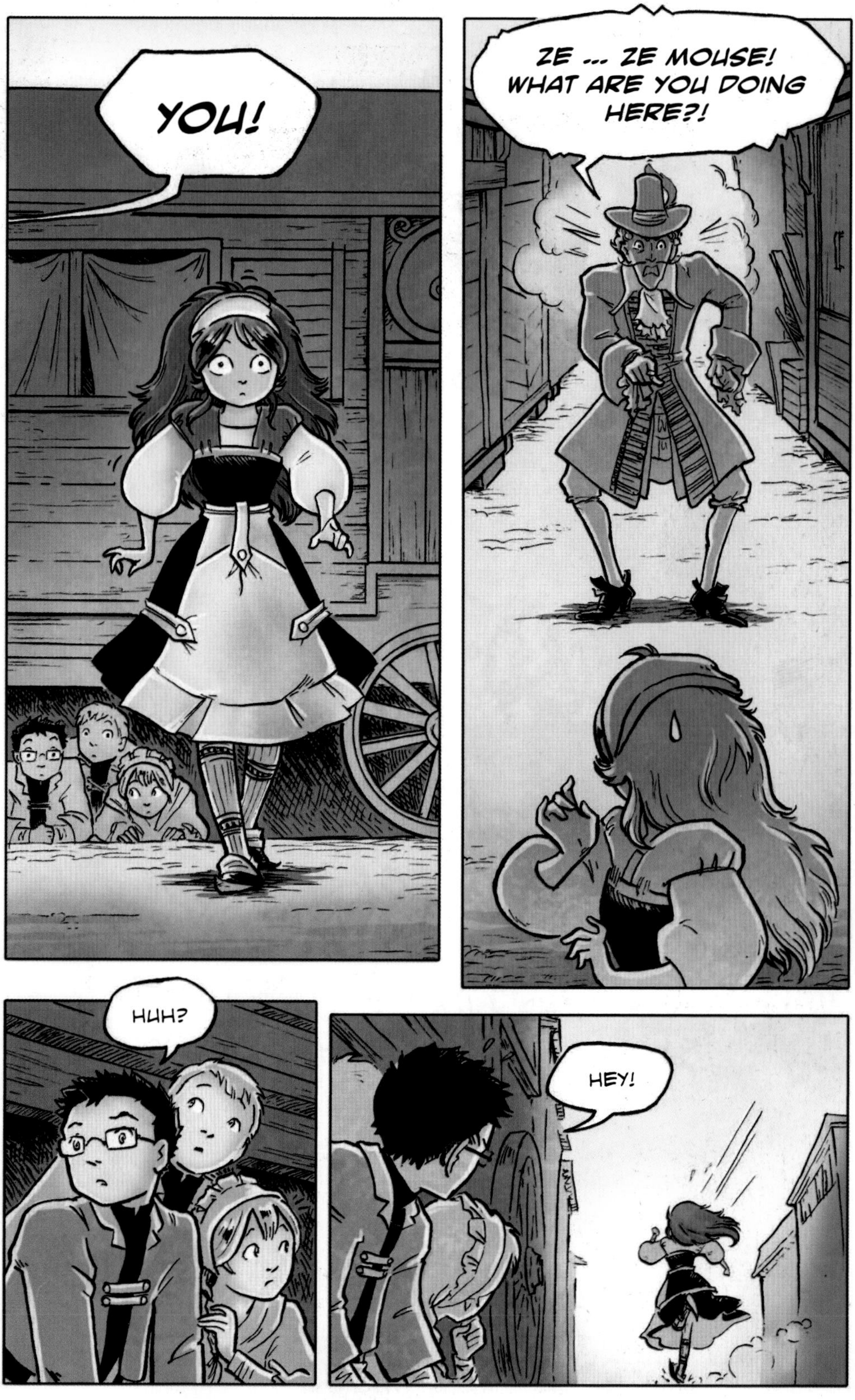
YOU!
ZE ... ZE MOUSE! WHAT ARE YOU DOING HERE?!
HUH?
HEY!

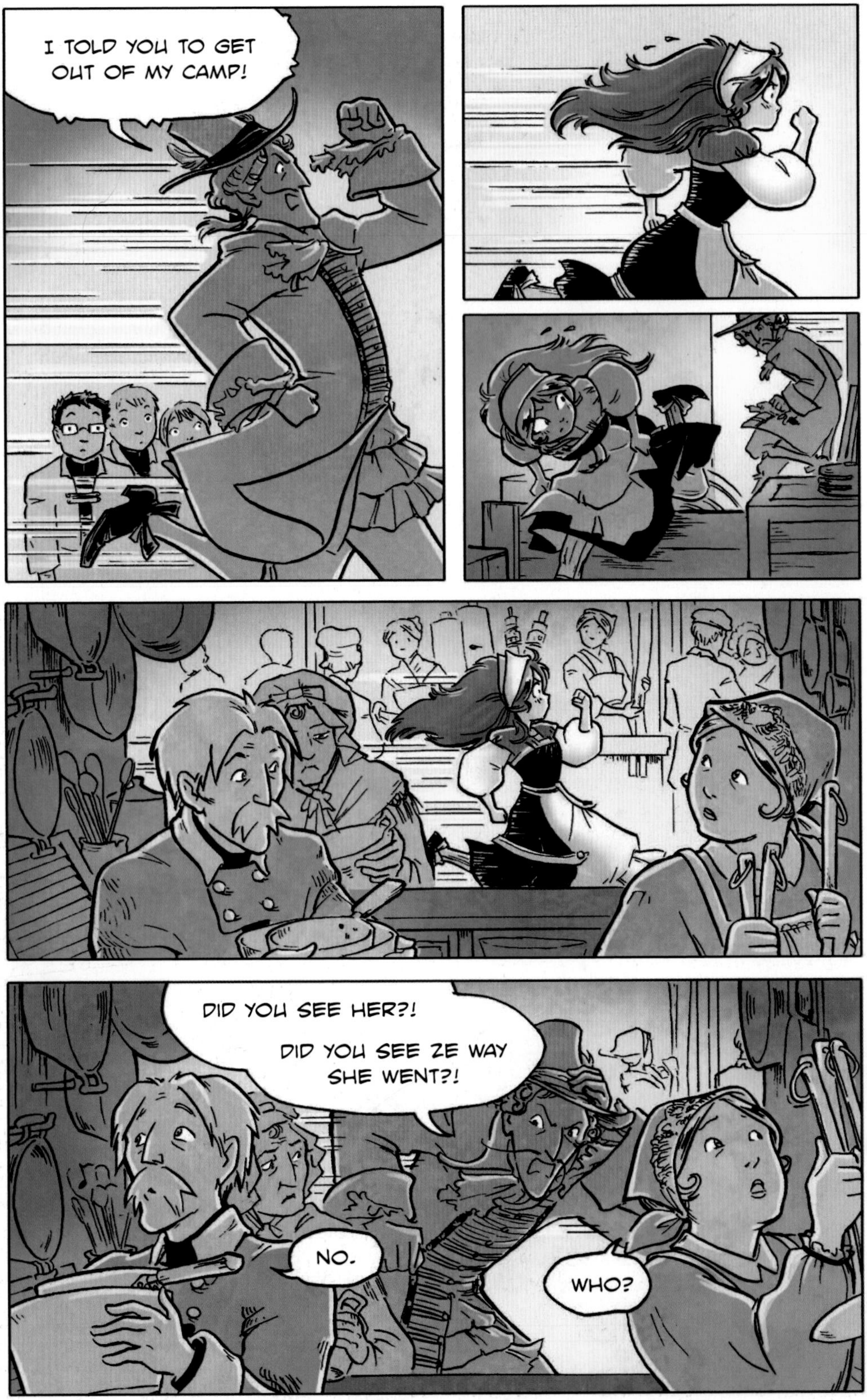
I TOLD YOU TO GET OUT OF MY CAMP!
DID YOU SEE HER?!
DID YOU SEE ZE WAY SHE WENT?!
NO.
WHO?

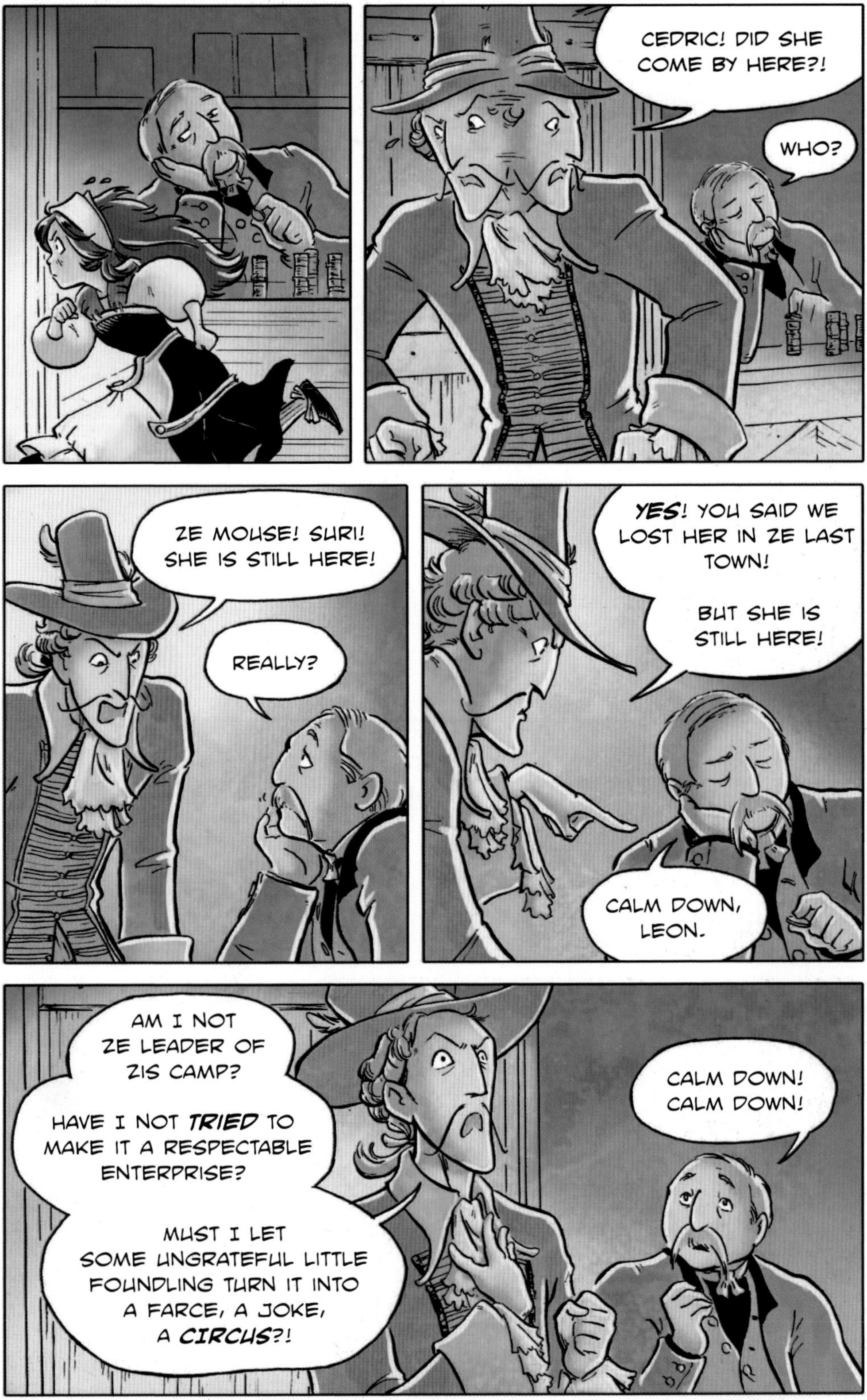
CEDRIC! DID SHE COME BY HERE?!
WHO?
ZE MOUSE! SURI! SHE IS STILL HERE!
REALLY?
YES! YOU SAID WE LOST HER IN ZE LAST TOWN!
BUT SHE IS STILL HERE!
CALM DOWN, LEON.
AM I NOT ZE LEADER OF ZIS CAMP?
HAVE I NOT TRIED TO MAKE IT A RESPECTABLE ENTERPRISE?
MUST I LET SOME UNGRATEFUL LITTLE FOUNDLING TURN IT INTO A FARCE, A JOKE, A CIRCUS?!
CALM DOWN! CALM DOWN!

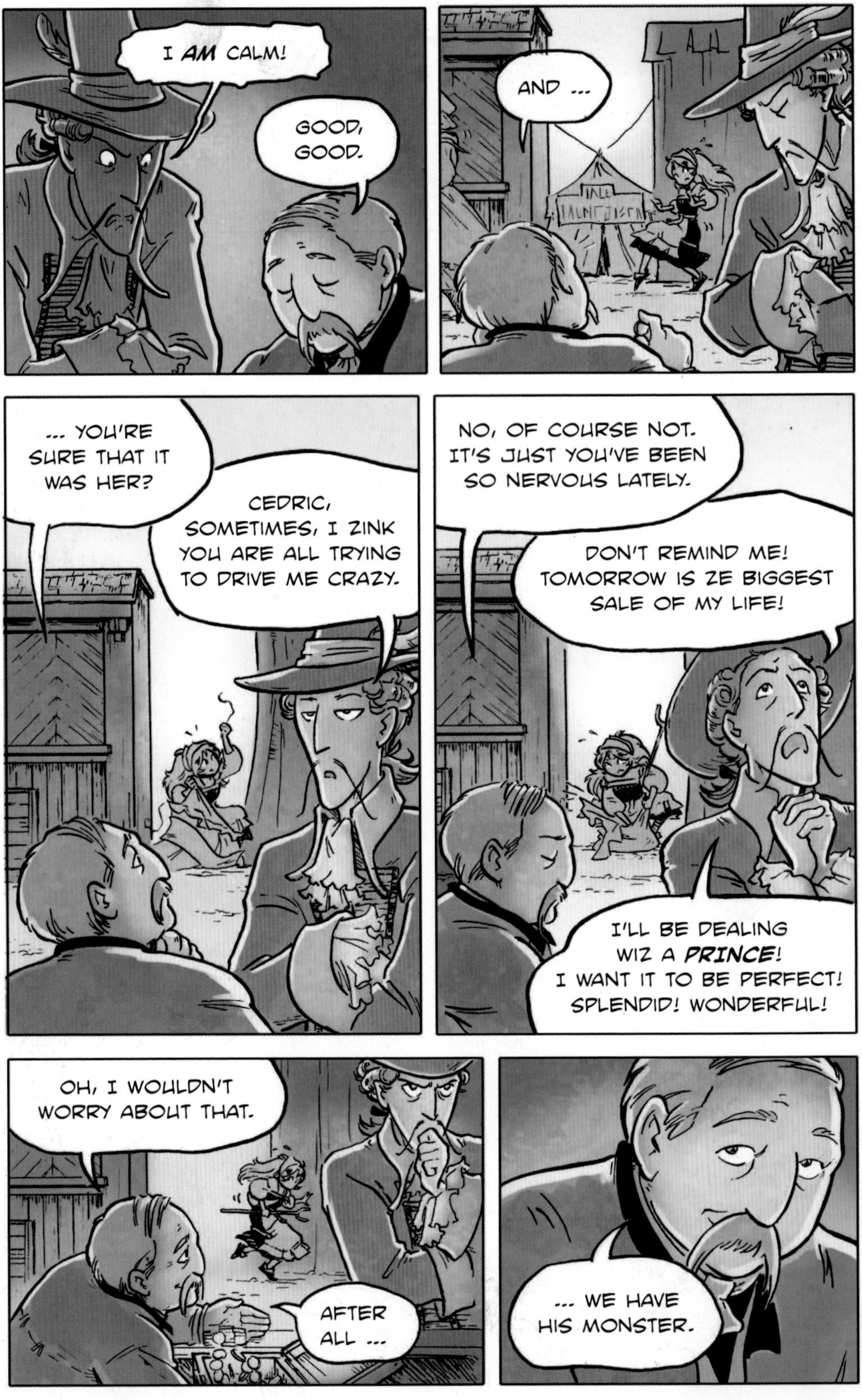
I AM CALM!
GOOD, GOOD.
AND ...
... YOU'RE SURE THAT IT WAS HER?
CEDRIC, SOMETIMES, I ZINK YOU ARE ALL TRYING TO DRIVE ME CRAZY.
NO, OF COURSE NOT. IT'S JUST YOU'VE BEEN SO NERVOUS LATELY.
DON'T REMIND ME! TOMORROW IS ZE BIGGEST SALE OF MY LIFE!
I'LL BE DEALING WIZ A PRINCE! I WANT IT TO BE PERFECT! SPLENDID! WONDERFUL!
OH, I WOULDN'T WORRY ABOUT THAT.
AFTER ALL ...
... WE HAVE HIS MONSTER.

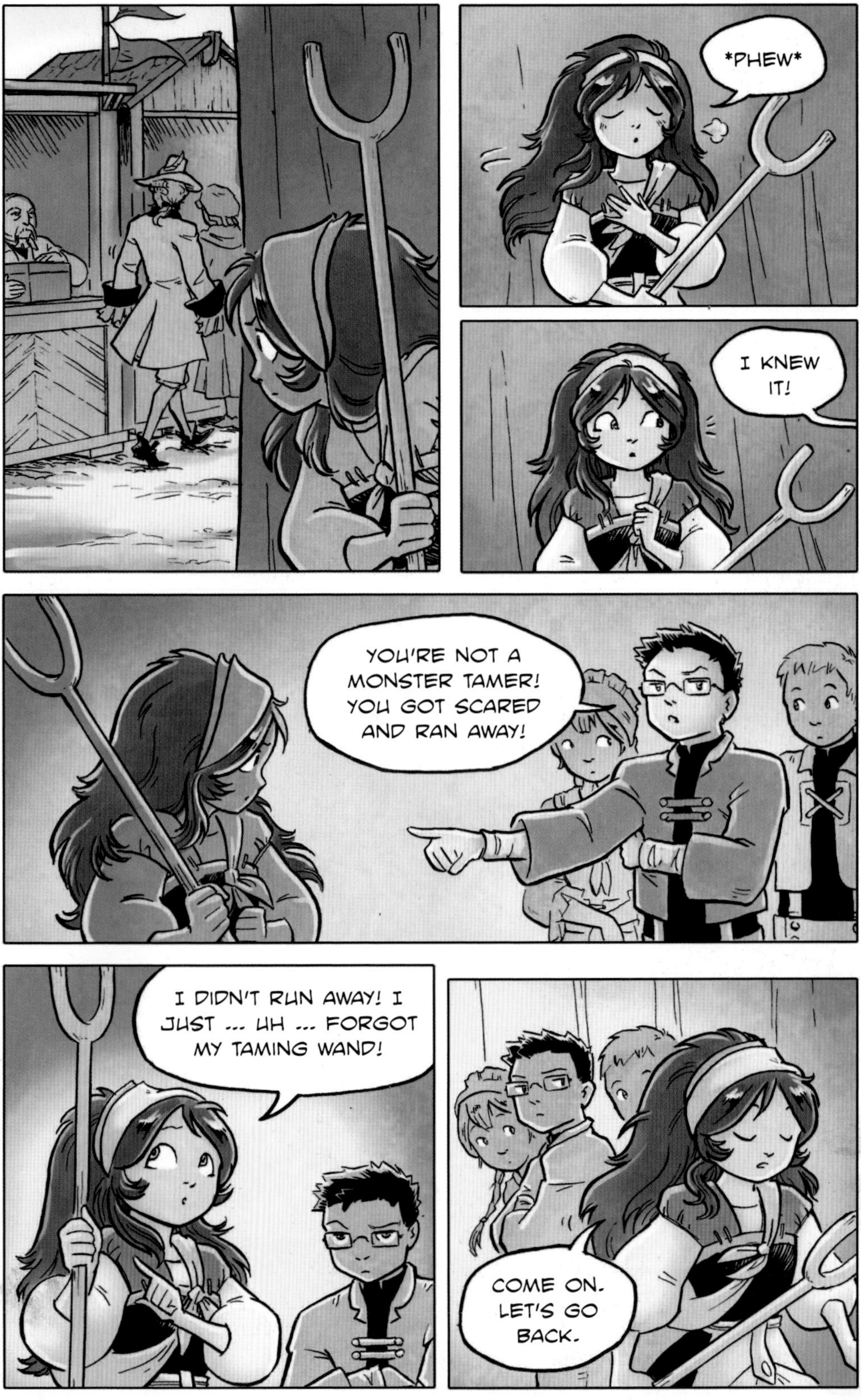
PHEW
I KNEW IT!
YOU'RE NOT A MONSTER TAMER! YOU GOT SCARED AND RAN AWAY!
I DIDN'T RUN AWAY! I JUST ... UH ... FORGOT MY TAMING WAND!
COME ON. LET'S GO BACK.

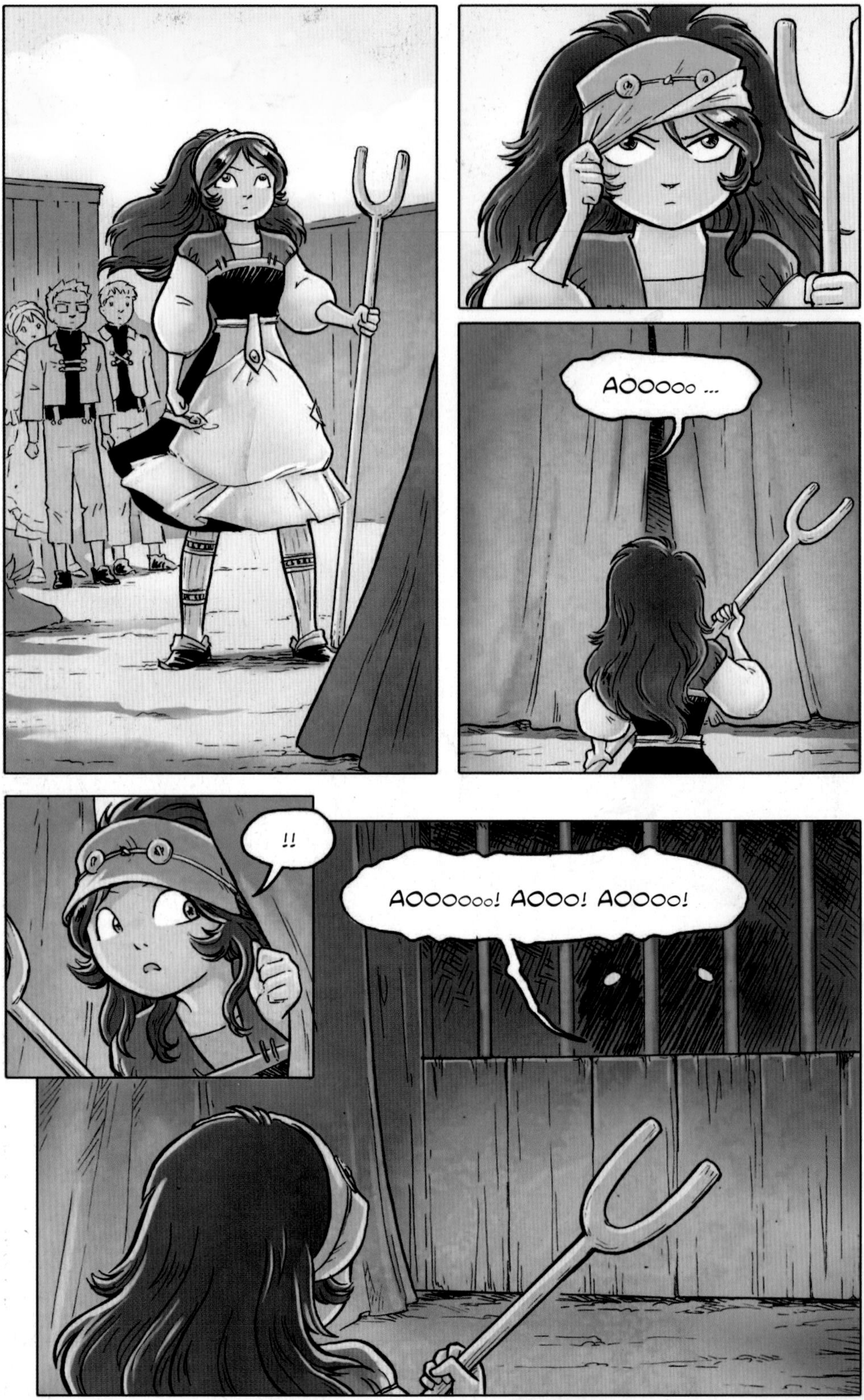
AOOOoo ...
!!
AOOOooo! AOOO! AOOOo!

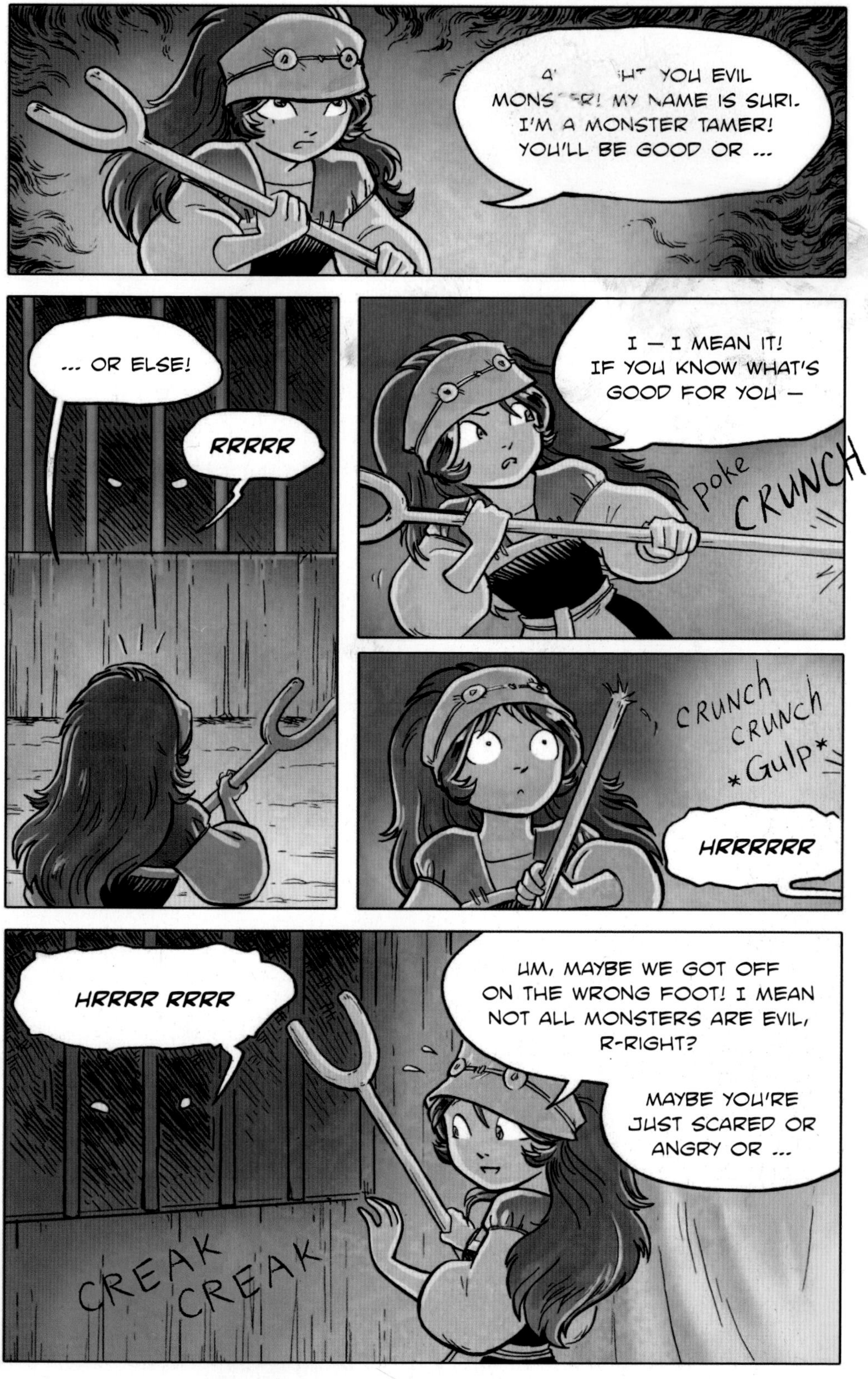
YOU EVIL
MY NAME IS SURI.
I'M A MONSTER TAMER!
YOU'LL BE GOOD OR ...
... OR ELSE!
RRRRR
I — I MEAN IT! IF YOU KNOW WHAT'S GOOD FOR YOU —
poke
CRUNCH
CRUNCH
CRUNCH
Gulp
HRRRRRR
HRRRR RRRR
UM, MAYBE WE GOT OFF ON THE WRONG FOOT! I MEAN NOT ALL MONSTERS ARE EVIL, R-RIGHT?
MAYBE YOU'RE JUST SCARED OR ANGRY OR ...
CREAK
CREAK

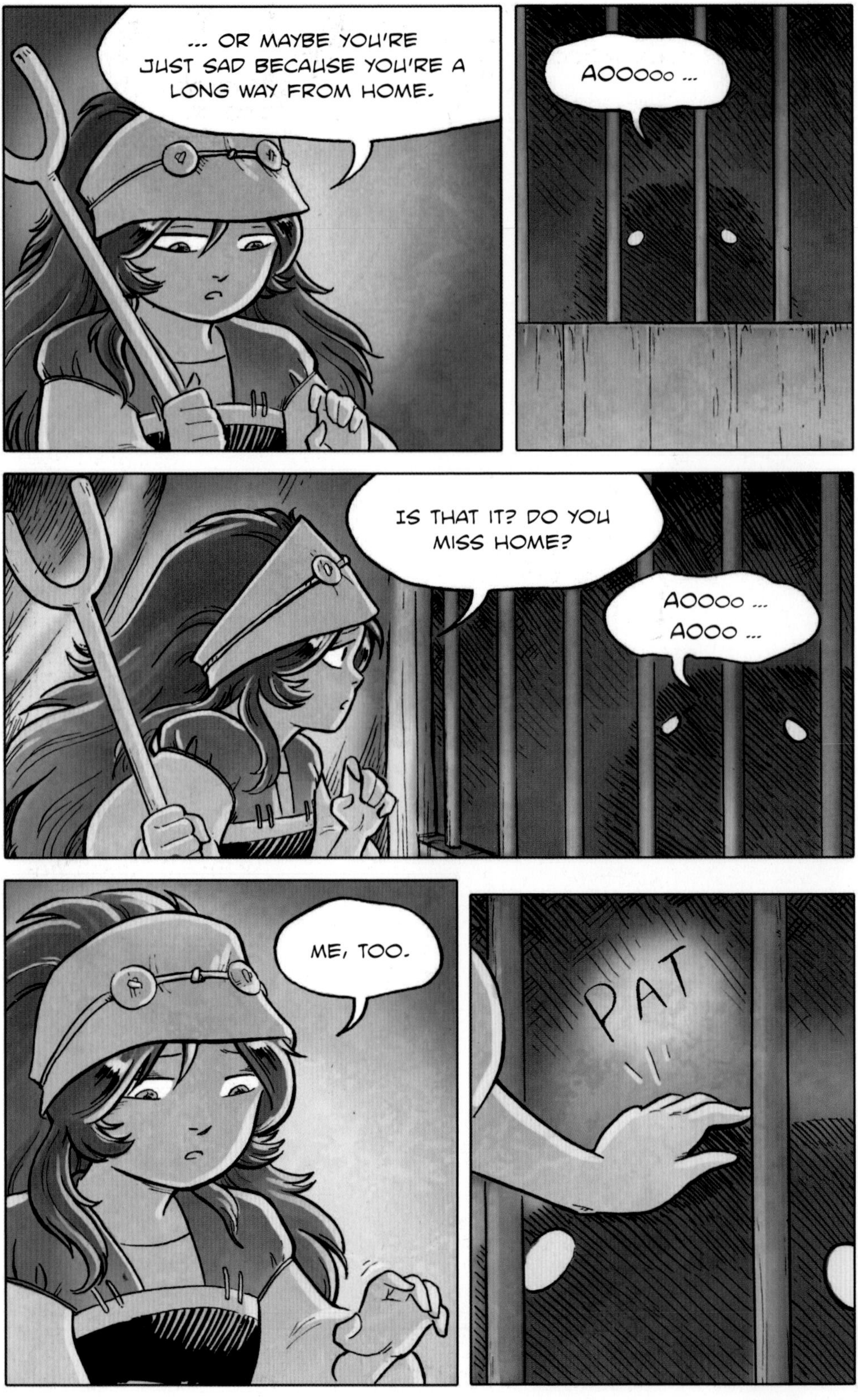

... OR MAYBE YOU'RE JUST SAD BECAUSE YOU'RE A LONG WAY FROM HOME.
AOOooo ...
IS THAT IT? DO YOU MISS HOME?
AOOoo ... AOOo ...
ME, TOO.
PAT

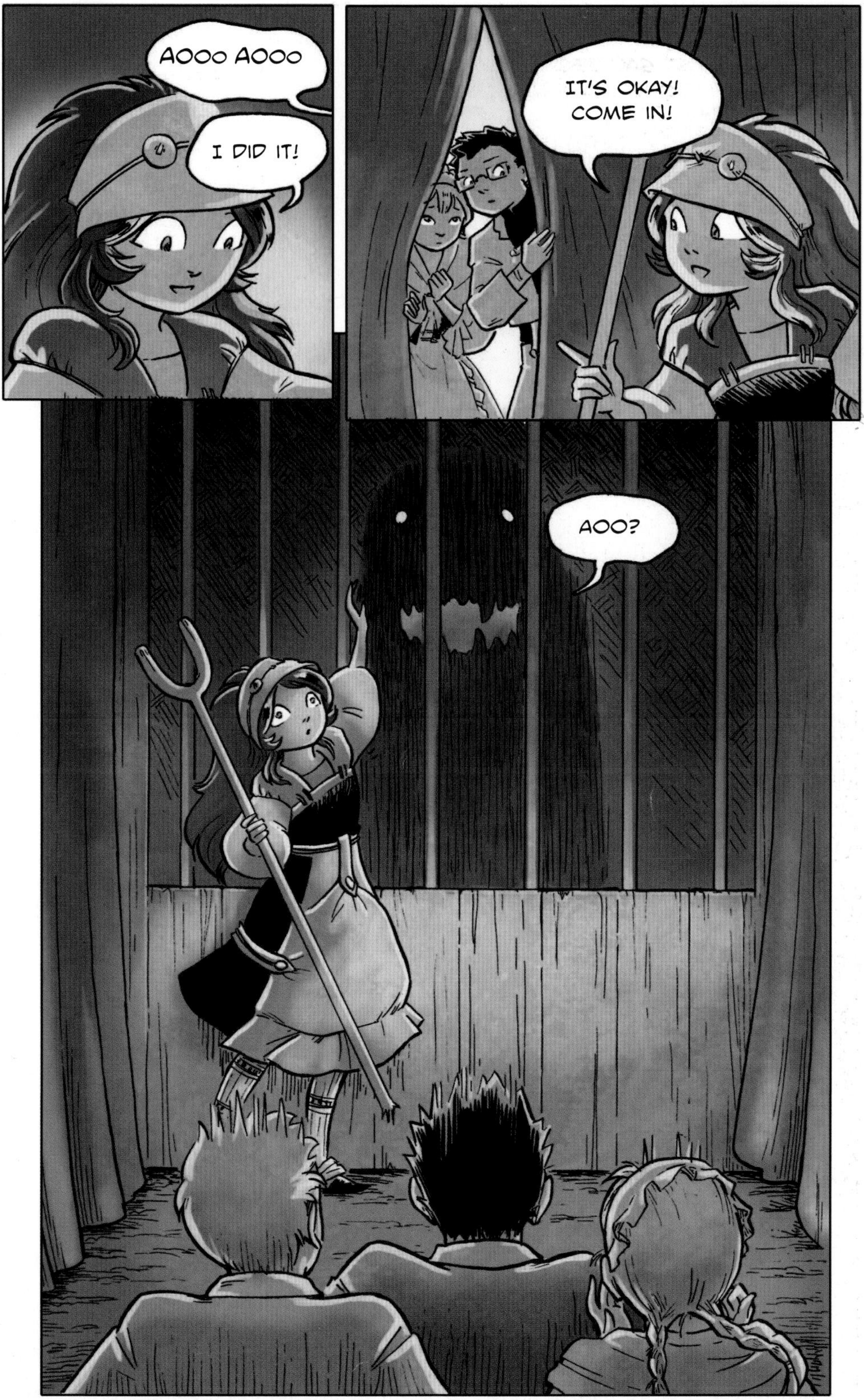
AOOo AOOo
I DID IT!
IT'S OKAY! COME IN!
AOO?

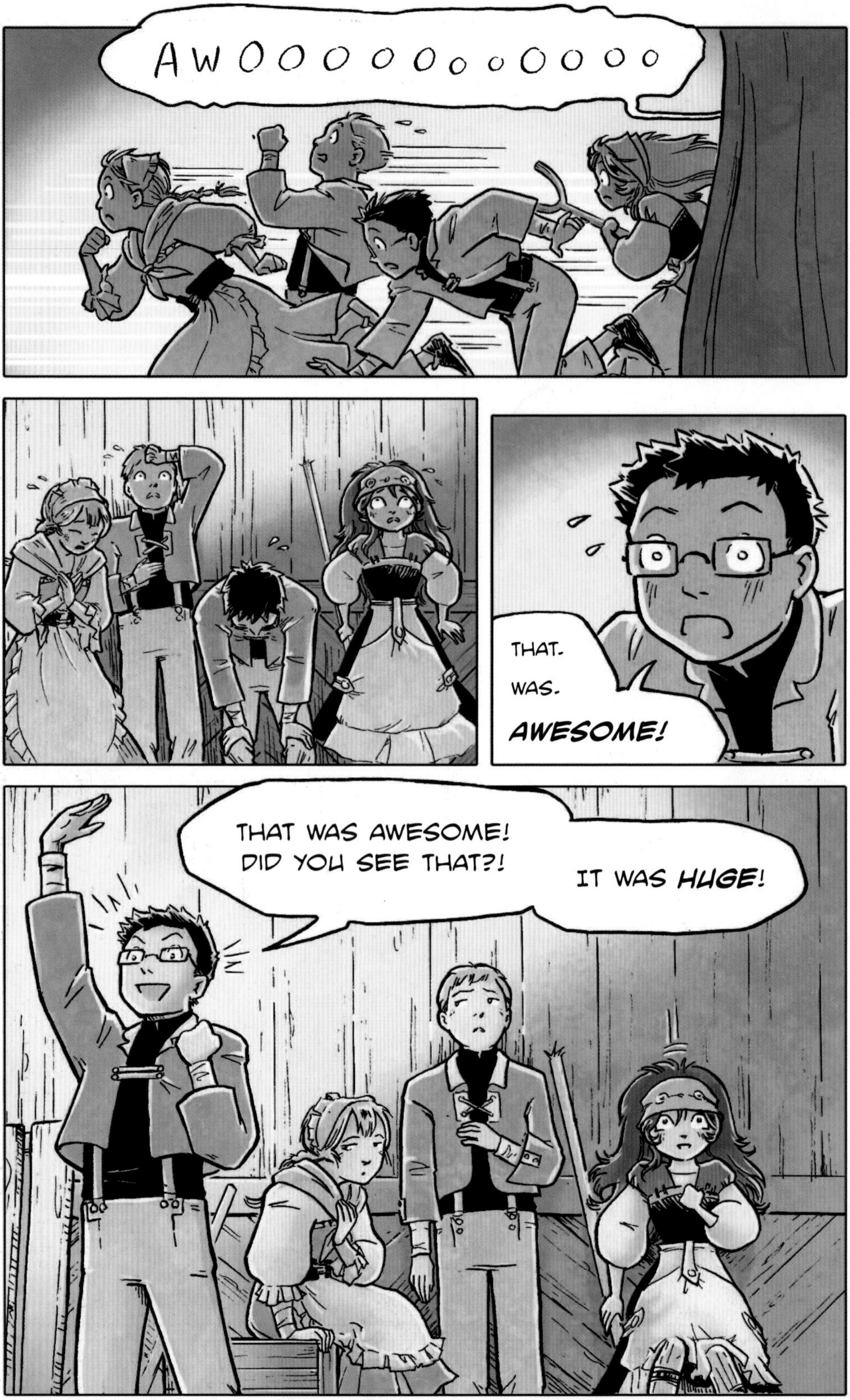
AWOOOOOOoOOOOO
THAT.
WAS.
AWESOME!
THAT WAS AWESOME! DID YOU SEE THAT?!
IT WAS HUGE!

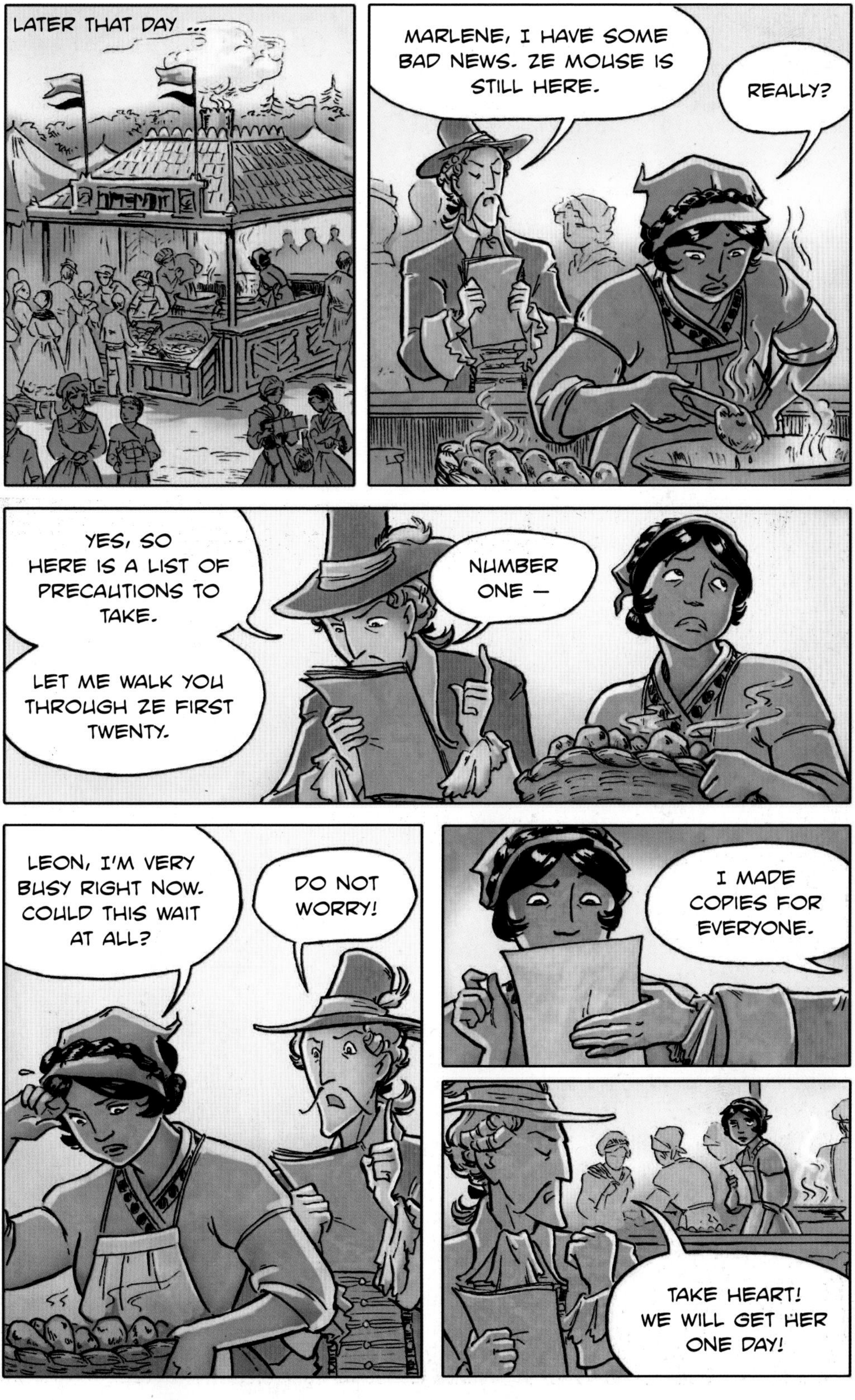
LATER THAT DAY ...
MARLENE, I HAVE SOME BAD NEWS. ZE MOUSE IS STILL HERE.
REALLY?
YES, SO HERE IS A LIST OF PRECAUTIONS TO TAKE.
LET ME WALK YOU THROUGH ZE FIRST TWENTY.
NUMBER ONE —
LEON, I'M VERY BUSY RIGHT NOW. COULD THIS WAIT AT ALL?
DO NOT WORRY!
I MADE COPIES FOR EVERYONE.
TAKE HEART! WE WILL GET HER ONE DAY!

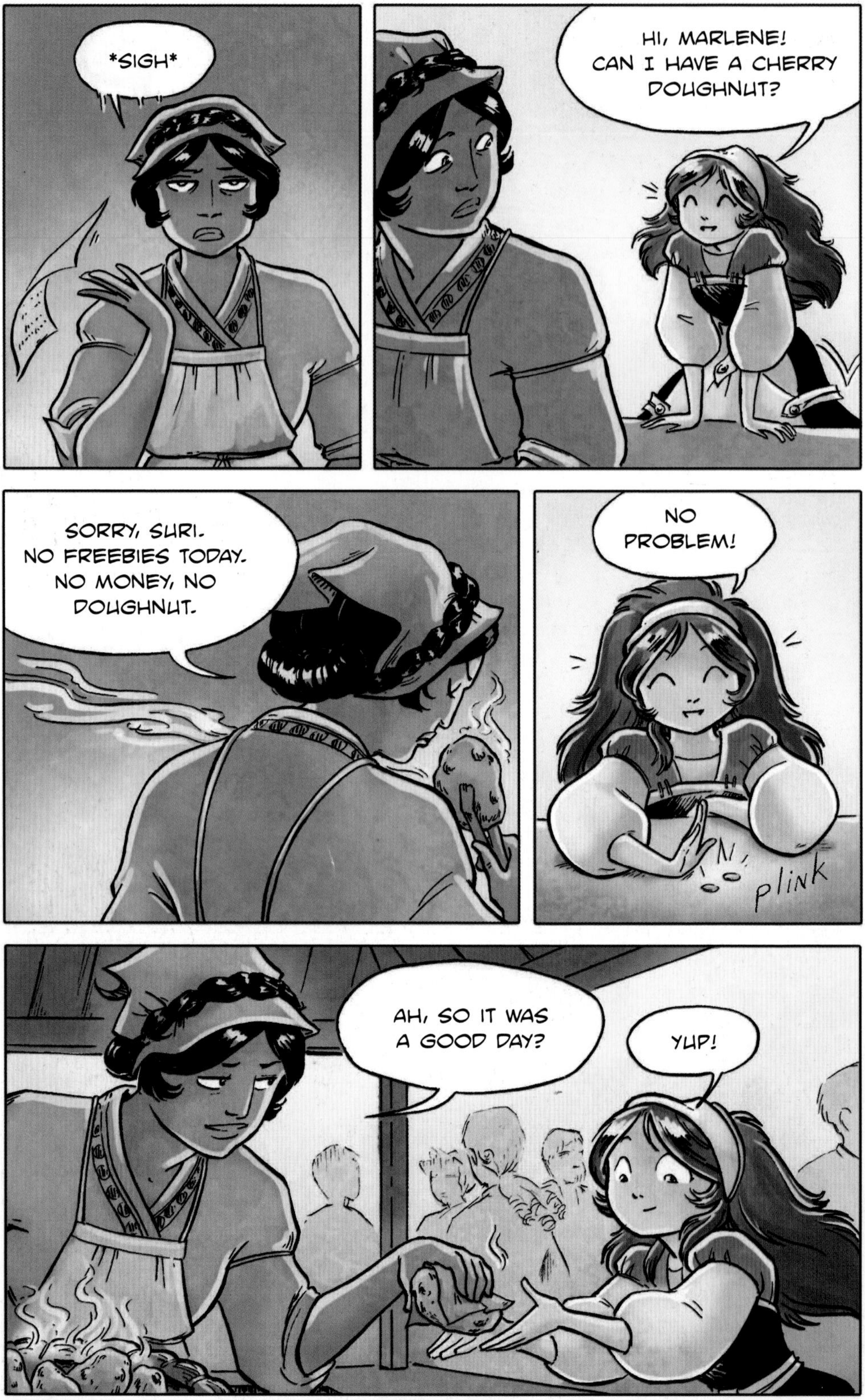
SIGH
HI, MARLENE! CAN I HAVE A CHERRY DOUGHNUT?
SORRY, SURI. NO FREEBIES TODAY. NO MONEY, NO DOUGHNUT.
NO PROBLEM!
plink
AH, SO IT WAS A GOOD DAY?
YUP!

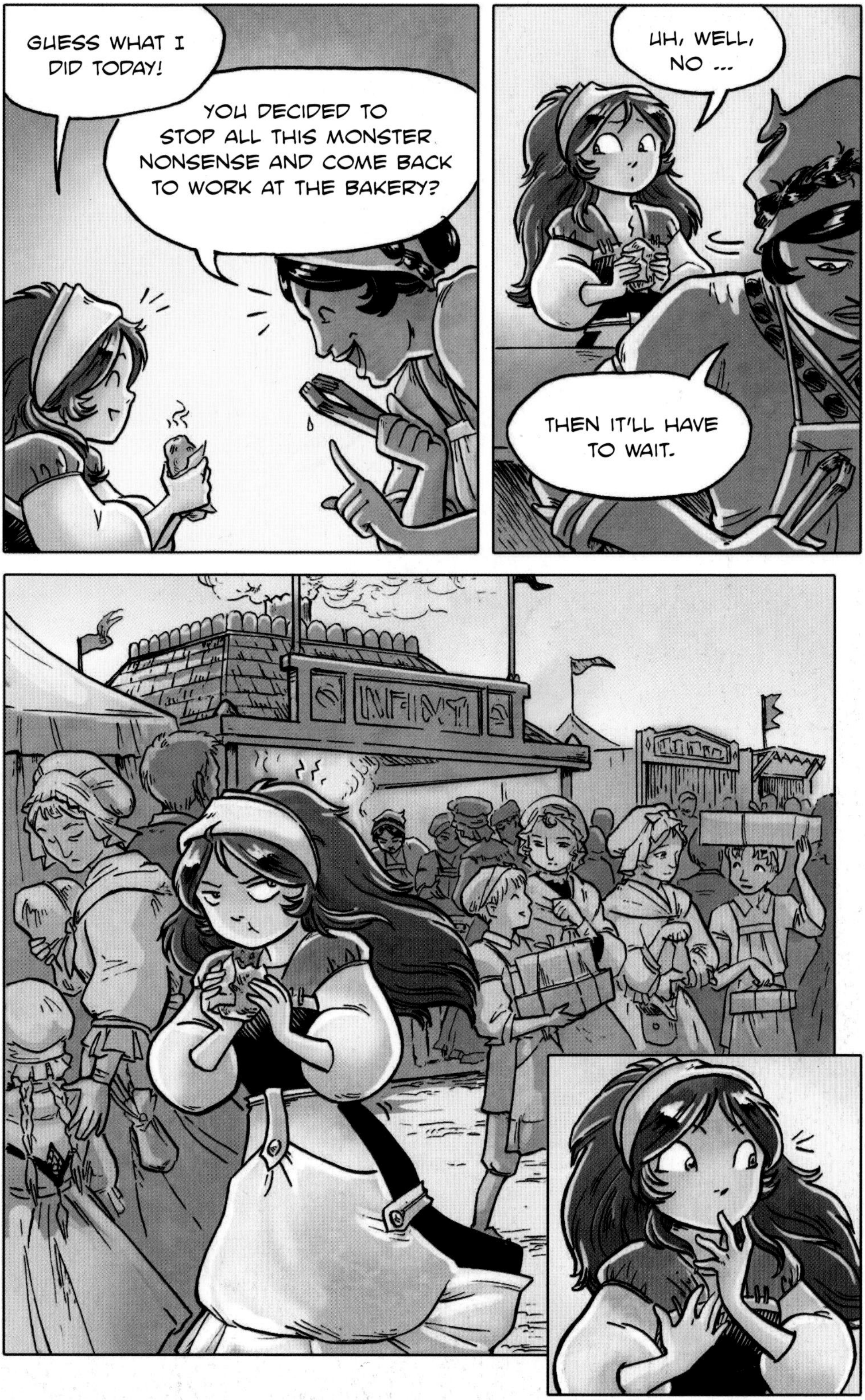
GUESS WHAT I DID TODAY!
YOU DECIDED TO STOP ALL THIS MONSTER NONSENSE AND COME BACK TO WORK AT THE BAKERY?
UH, WELL, NO ...
THEN IT'LL HAVE TO WAIT.

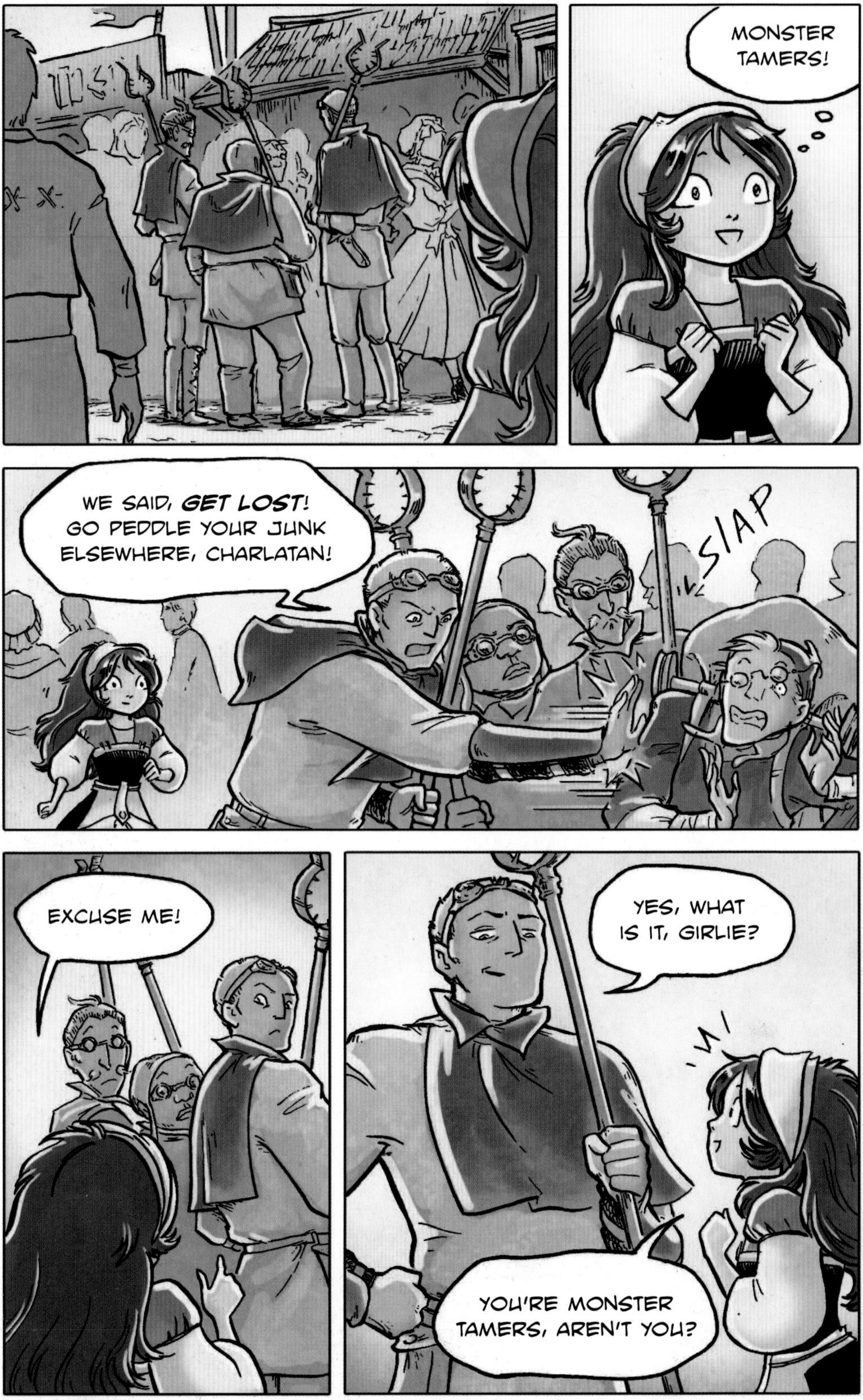
MONSTER TAMERS!
WE SAID, GET LOST! GO PEDDLE YOUR JUNK ELSEWHERE, CHARLATAN!
SLAP
EXCUSE ME!
YES, WHAT IS IT, GIRLIE?
YOU'RE MONSTER TAMERS, AREN'T YOU?

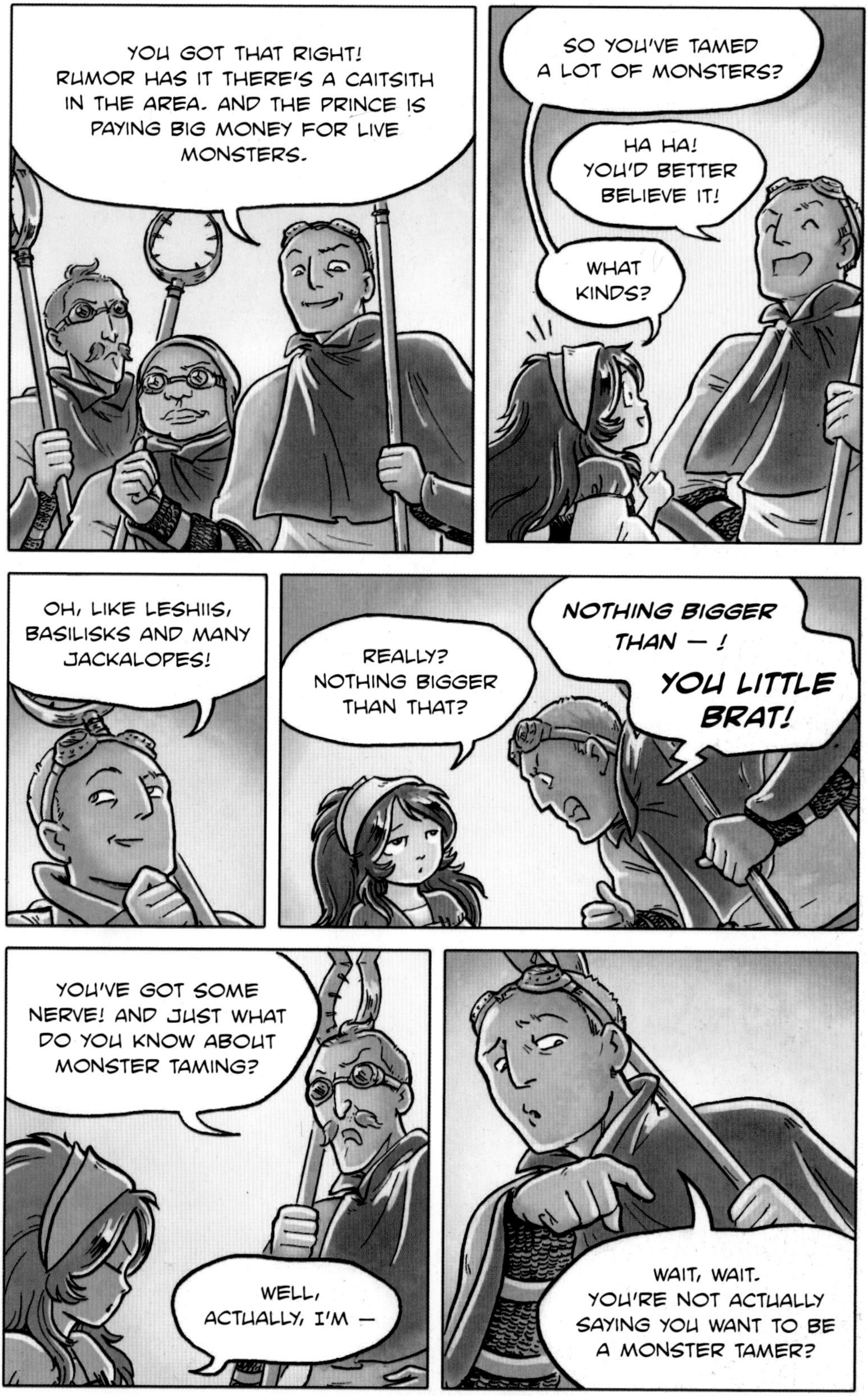
YOU GOT THAT RIGHT! RUMOR HAS IT THERE'S A CAITSITH IN THE AREA. AND THE PRINCE IS PAYING BIG MONEY FOR LIVE MONSTERS.
SO YOU'VE TAMED A LOT OF MONSTERS?
HA HA! YOU'D BETTER BELIEVE IT!
WHAT KINDS?
OH, LIKE LESHIIS, BASILISKS AND MANY JACKALOPES!
REALLY? NOTHING BIGGER THAN THAT?
NOTHING BIGGER THAN — !
YOU LITTLE BRAT!
YOU'VE GOT SOME NERVE! AND JUST WHAT DO YOU KNOW ABOUT MONSTER TAMING?
WELL, ACTUALLY, I'M —
WAIT, WAIT. YOU'RE NOT ACTUALLY SAYING YOU WANT TO BE A MONSTER TAMER?

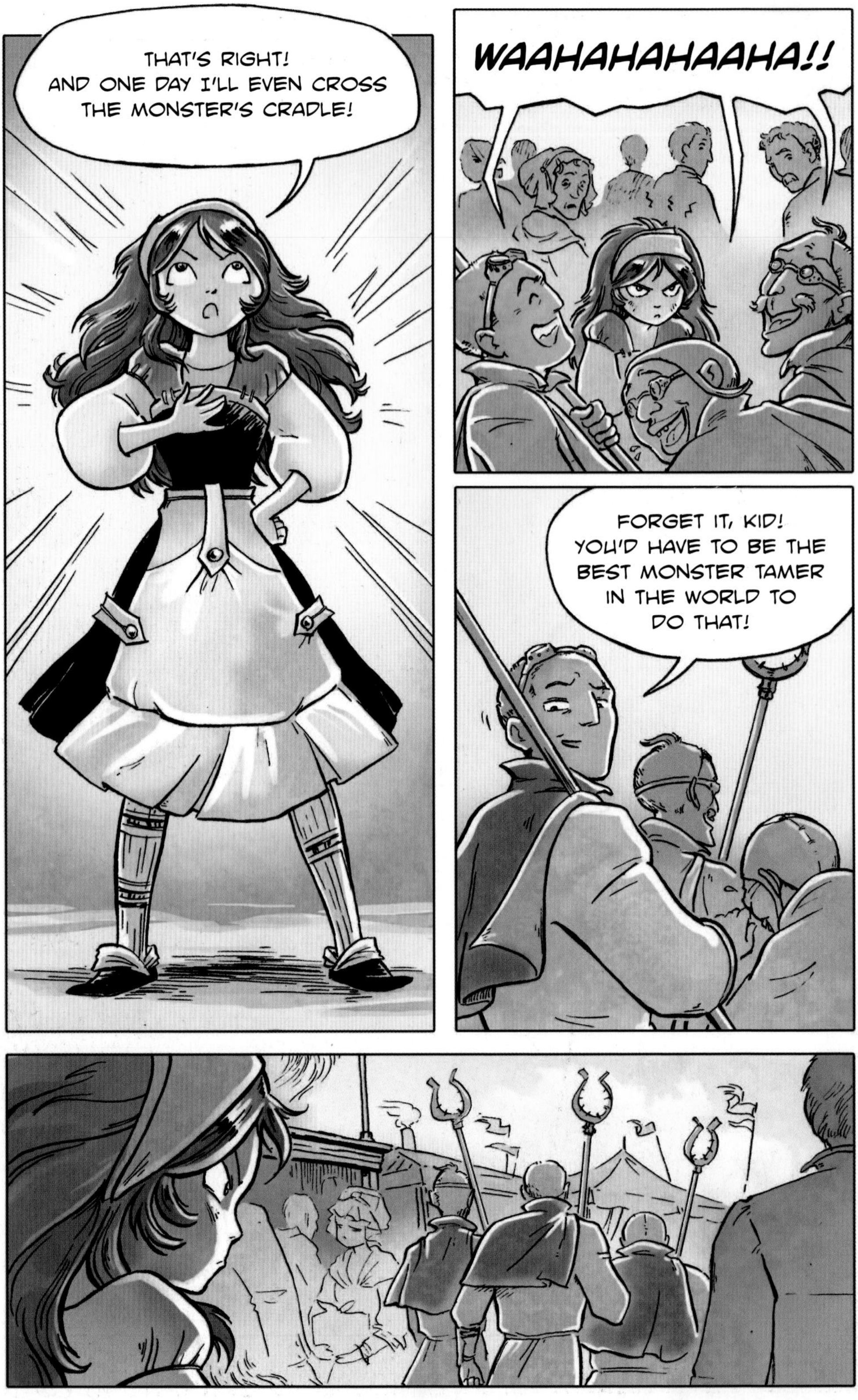
THAT'S RIGHT! AND ONE DAY I'LL EVEN CROSS THE MONSTER'S CRADLE!
WAAHAHAHAAHA!!
FORGET IT, KID! YOU'D HAVE TO BE THE BEST MONSTER TAMER IN THE WORLD TO DO THAT!

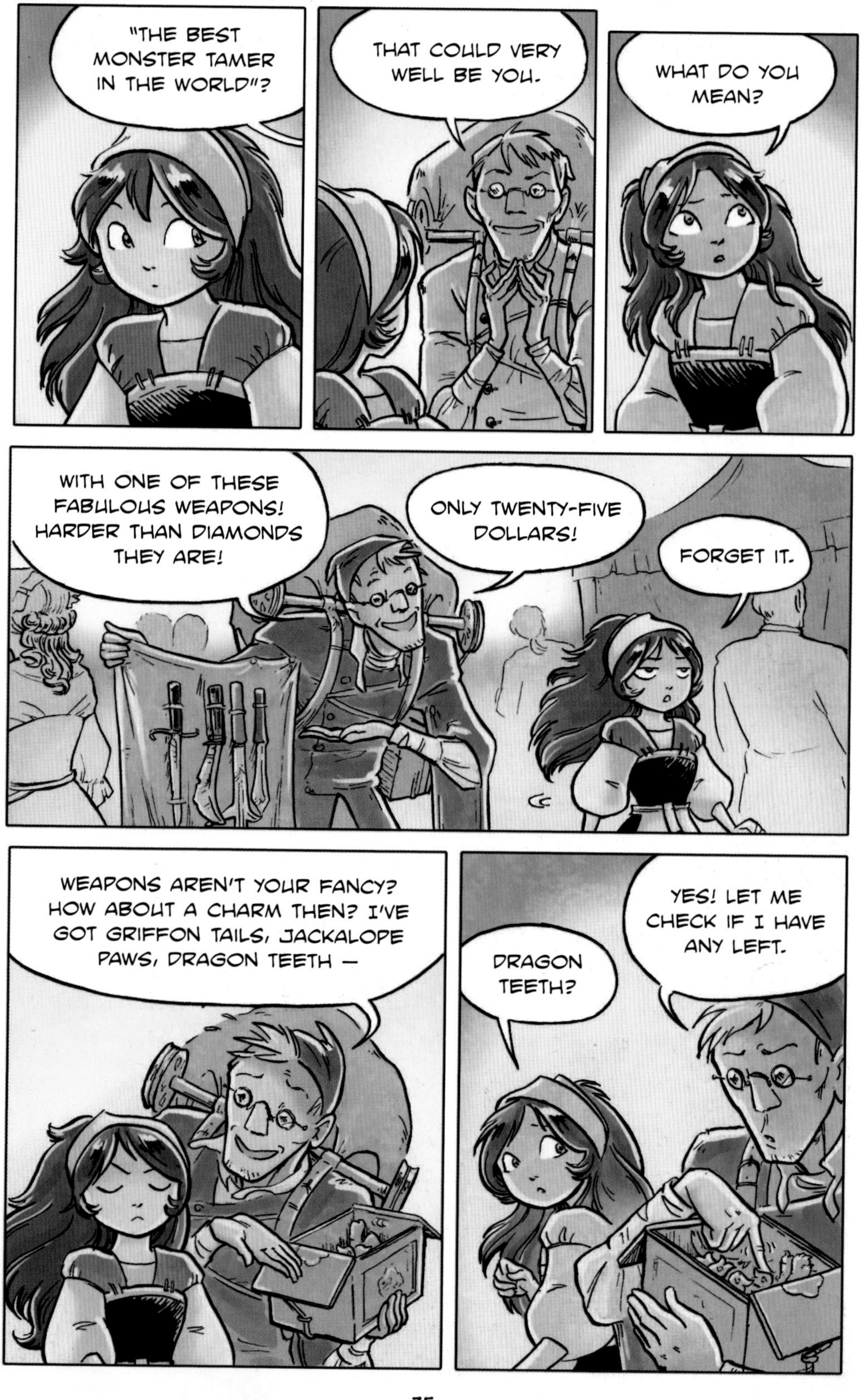
"THE BEST MONSTER TAMER IN THE WORLD"?
THAT COULD VERY WELL BE YOU.
WHAT DO YOU MEAN?
WITH ONE OF THESE FABULOUS WEAPONS! HARDER THAN DIAMONDS THEY ARE!
ONLY TWENTY-FIVE DOLLARS!
FORGET IT.
WEAPONS AREN'T YOUR FANCY? HOW ABOUT A CHARM THEN? I'VE GOT GRIFFON TAILS, JACKALOPE PAWS, DRAGON TEETH —
DRAGON TEETH?
YES! LET ME CHECK IF I HAVE ANY LEFT.

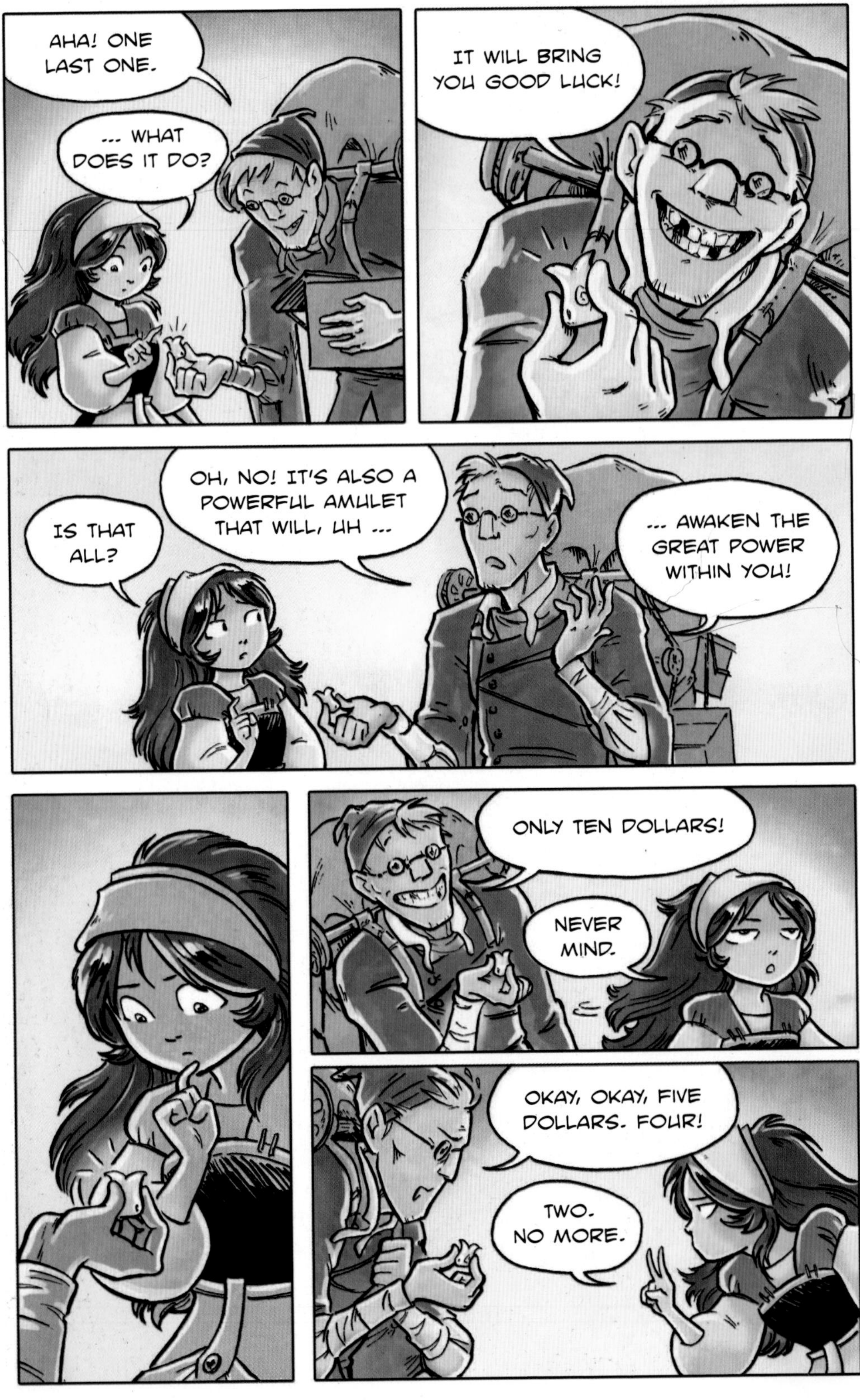

AHA! ONE LAST ONE.
... WHAT DOES IT DO?
IT WILL BRING YOU GOOD LUCK!
IS THAT ALL?
OH, NO! IT'S ALSO A POWERFUL AMULET THAT WILL, UH ...
... AWAKEN THE GREAT POWER WITHIN YOU!
ONLY TEN DOLLARS!
NEVER MIND.
OKAY, OKAY, FIVE DOLLARS. FOUR!
TWO. NO MORE.

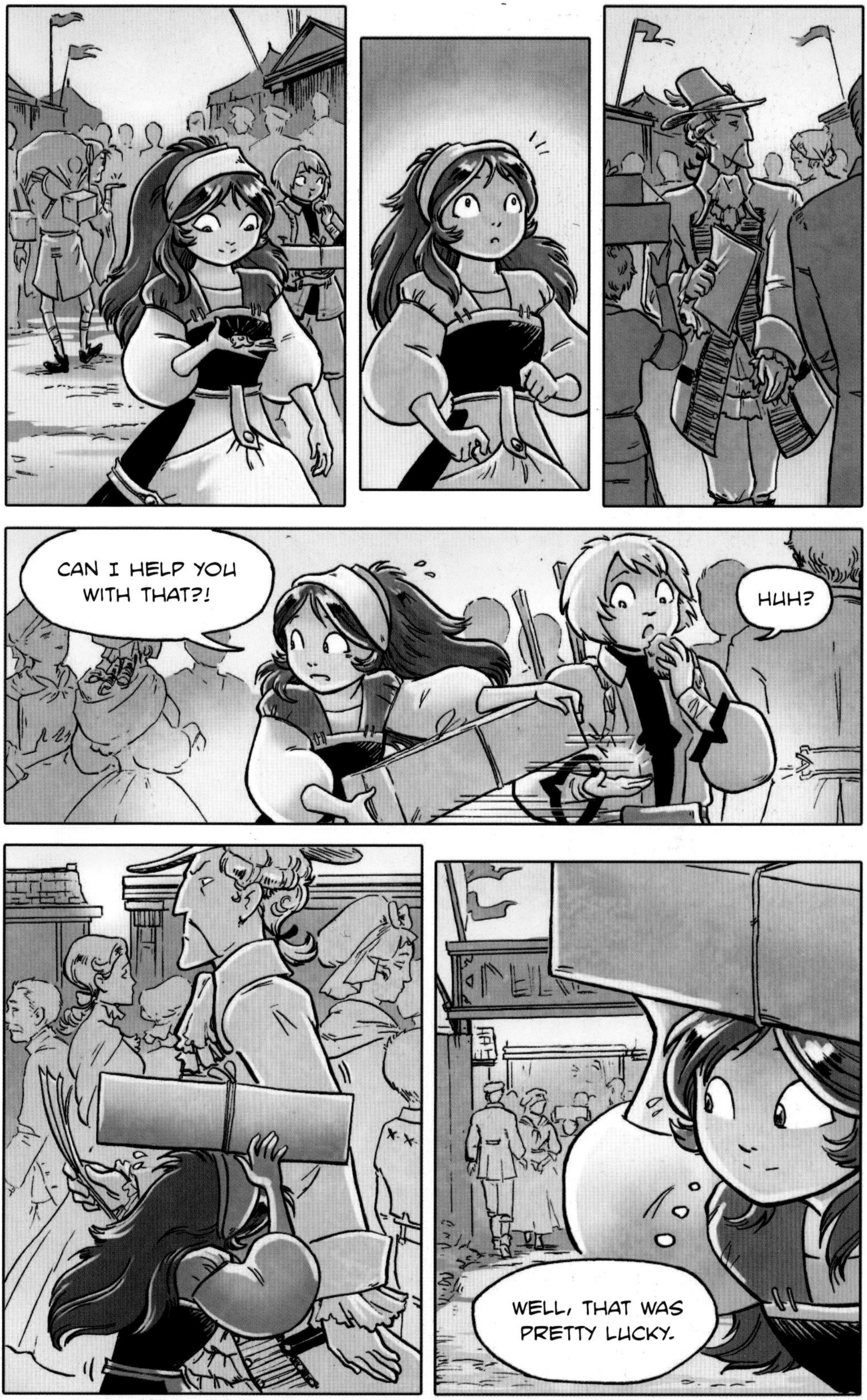
CAN I HELP YOU WITH THAT?!
HUH?
WELL, THAT WAS PRETTY LUCKY.

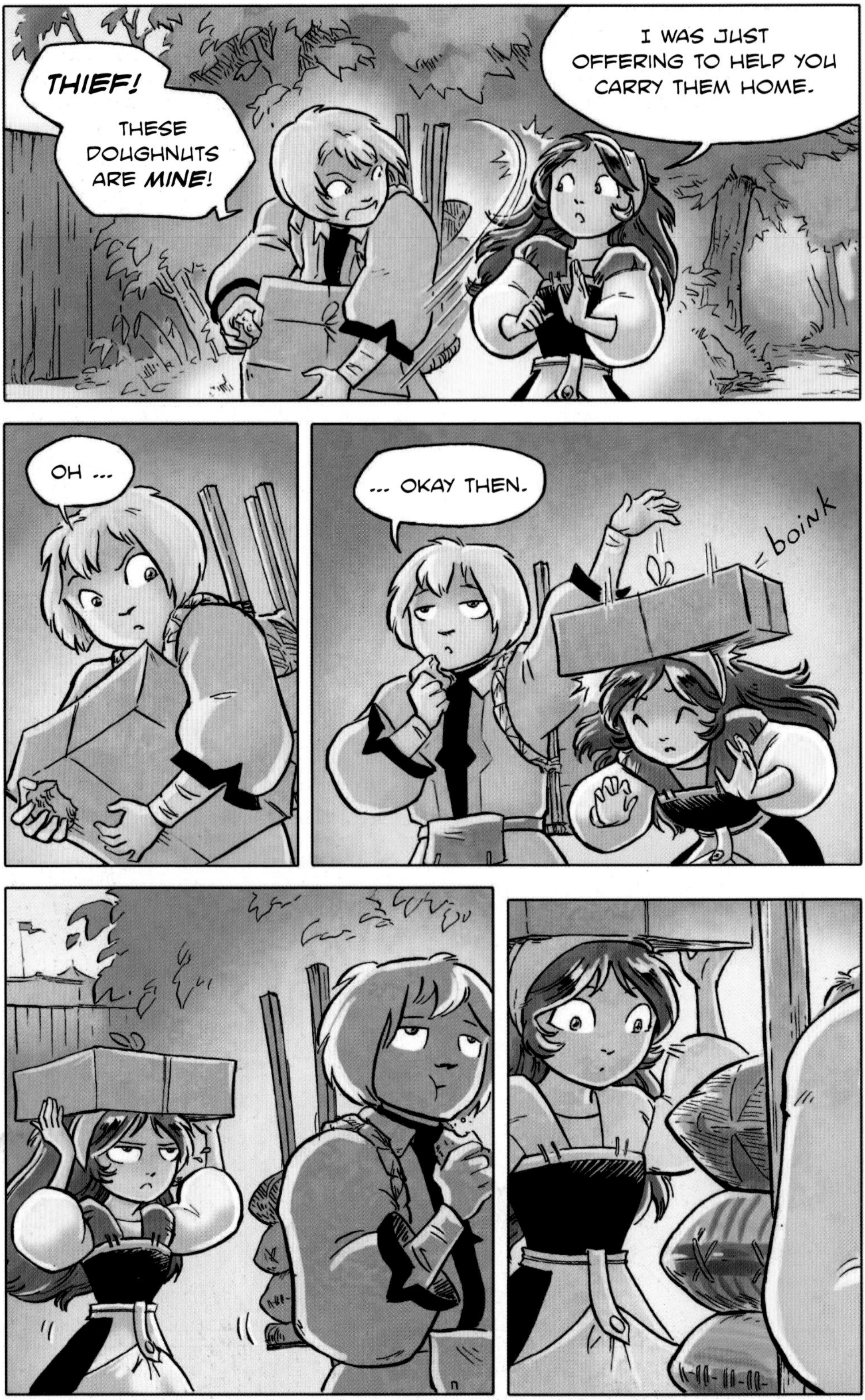
THIEF!
THESE DOUGHNUTS ARE MINE!
I WAS JUST OFFERING TO HELP YOU CARRY THEM HOME.
OH ...
... OKAY THEN.
boink

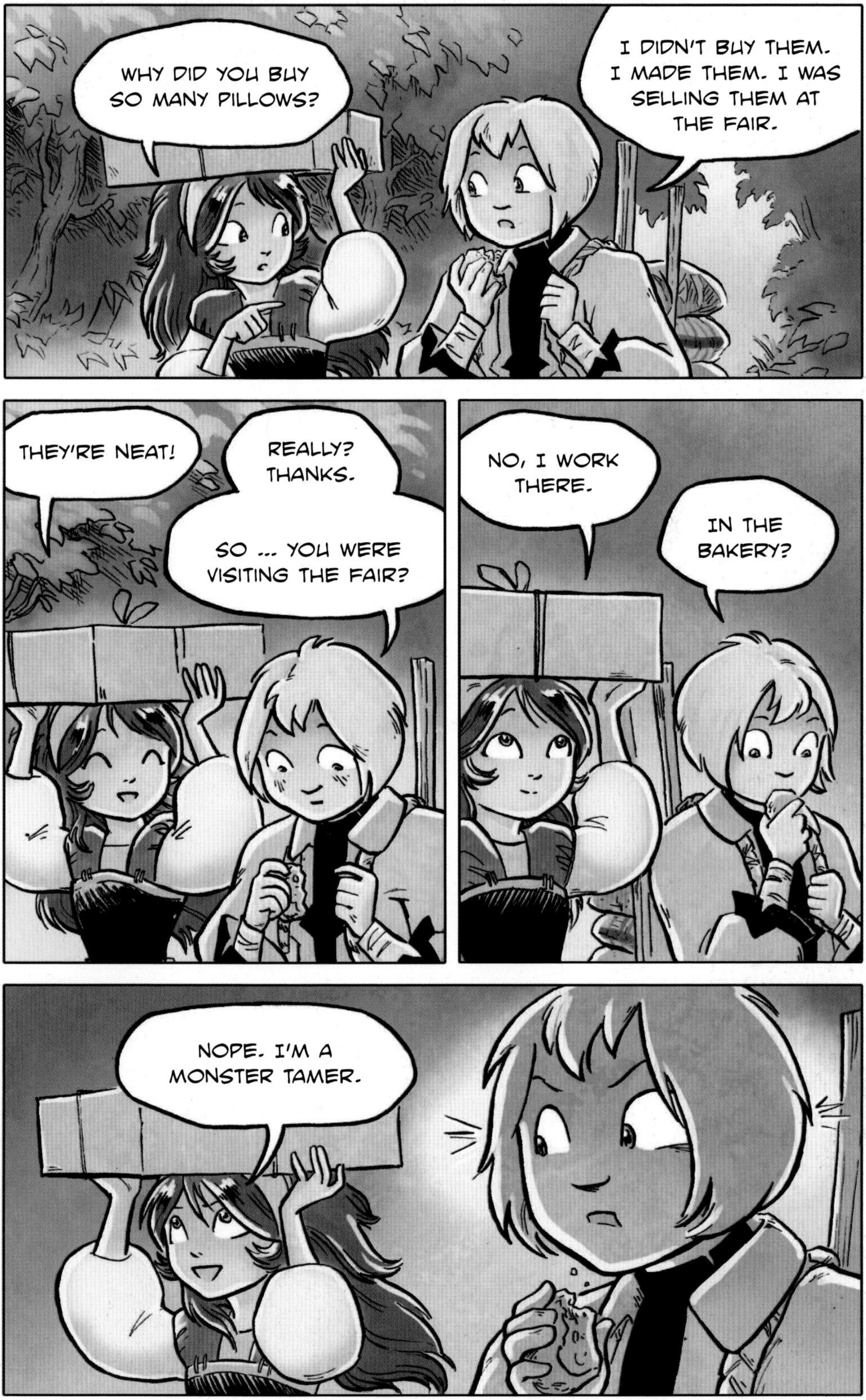
WHY DID YOU BUY SO MANY PILLOWS?
I DIDN'T BUY THEM. I MADE THEM. I WAS SELLING THEM AT THE FAIR.
THEY'RE NEAT!
REALLY? THANKS.
SO ... YOU WERE VISITING THE FAIR?
NO, I WORK THERE.
IN THE BAKERY?
NOPE. I'M A MONSTER TAMER.

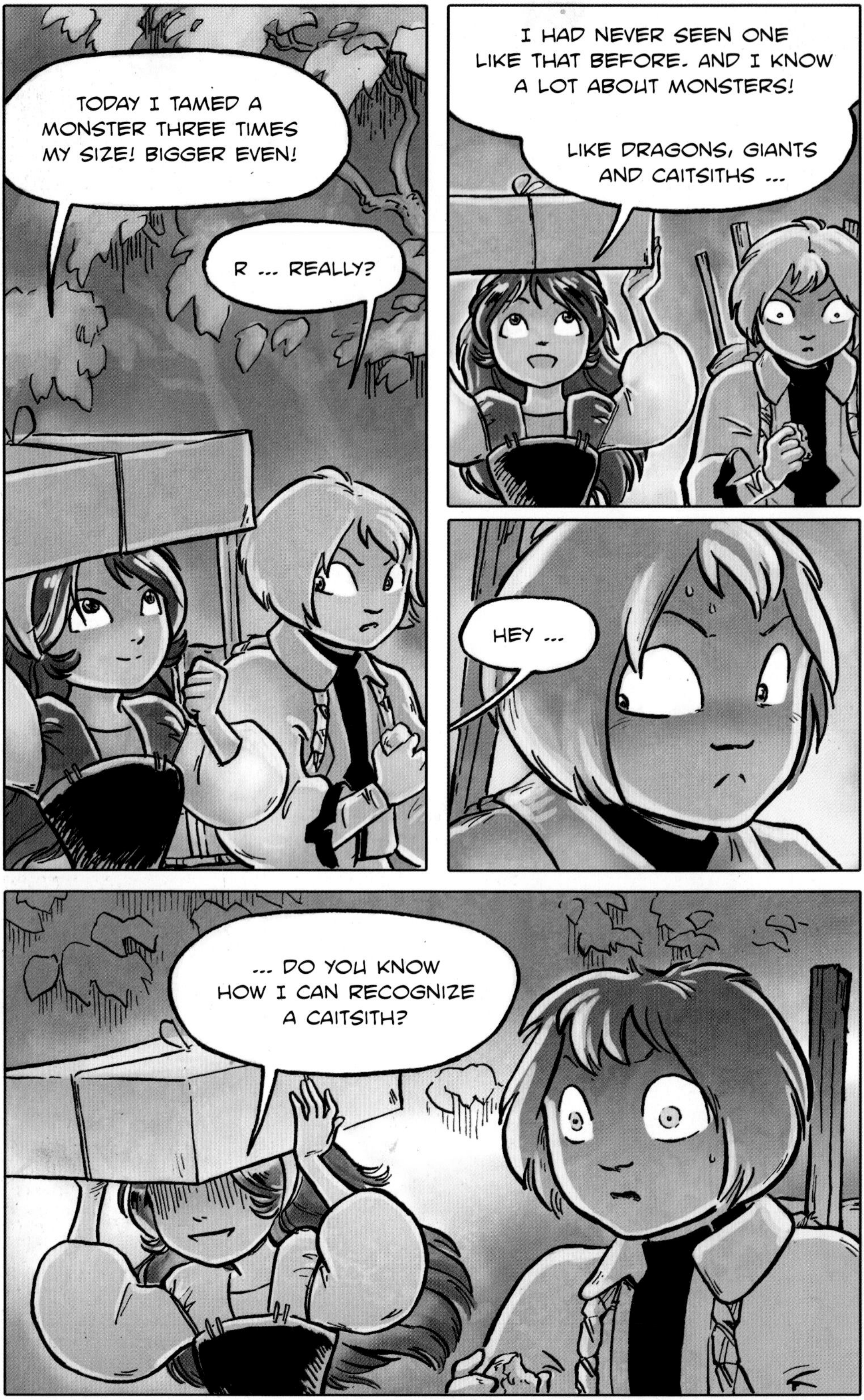
TODAY I TAMED A MONSTER THREE TIMES MY SIZE! BIGGER EVEN!
R ... REALLY?
I HAD NEVER SEEN ONE LIKE THAT BEFORE. AND I KNOW A LOT ABOUT MONSTERS!
LIKE DRAGONS, GIANTS AND CAITSITHS ...
HEY ...
... DO YOU KNOW HOW I CAN RECOGNIZE A CAITSITH?

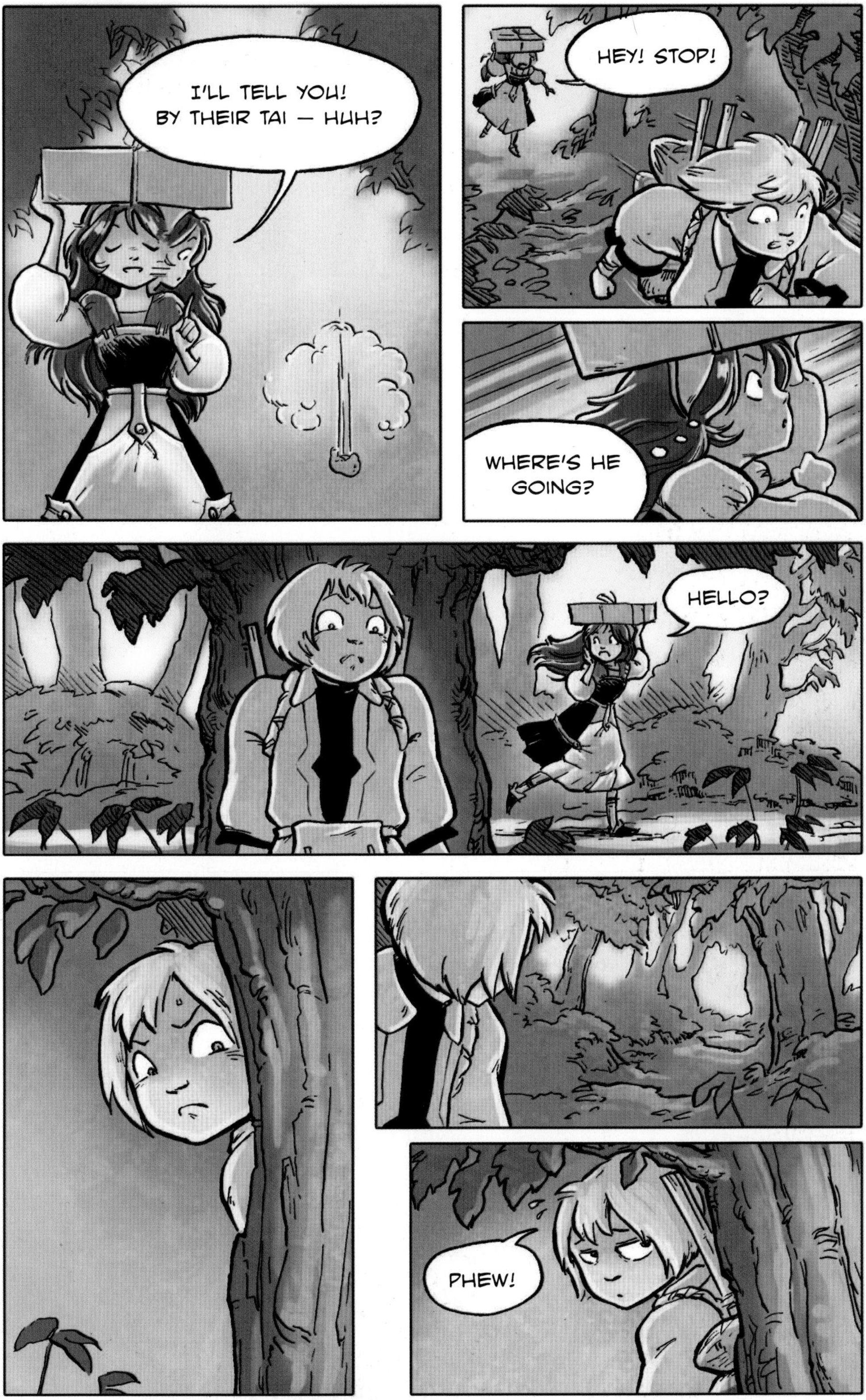
I'LL TELL YOU! BY THEIR TAI — HUH?
HEY! STOP!
WHERE'S HE GOING?
HELLO?
PHEW!

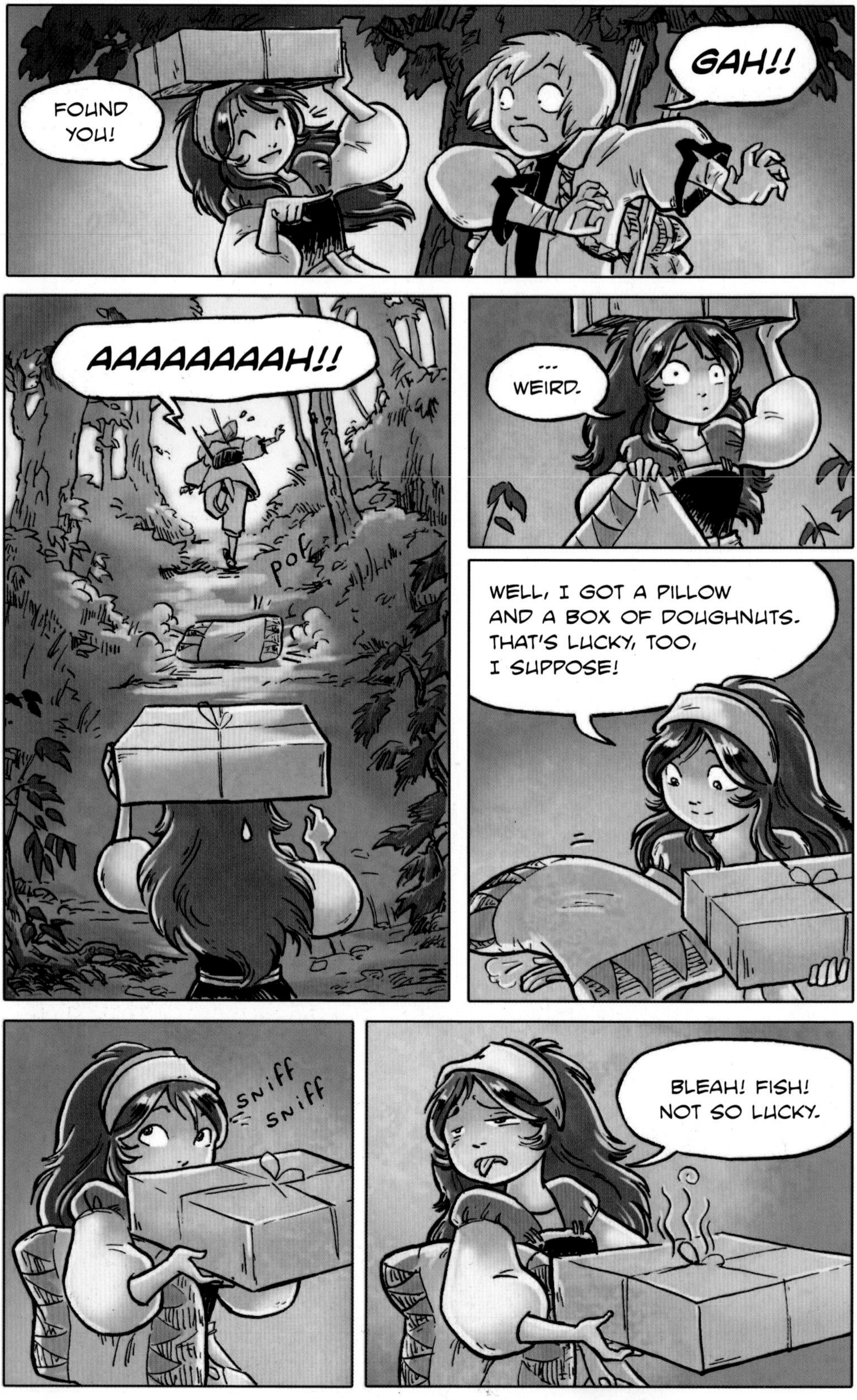
FOUND YOU!
GAH!!
AAAAAAAAH!!
pof
... WEIRD.
WELL, I GOT A PILLOW AND A BOX OF DOUGHNUTS. THAT'S LUCKY, TOO, I SUPPOSE!
sniff sniff
BLEAH! FISH! NOT SO LUCKY.

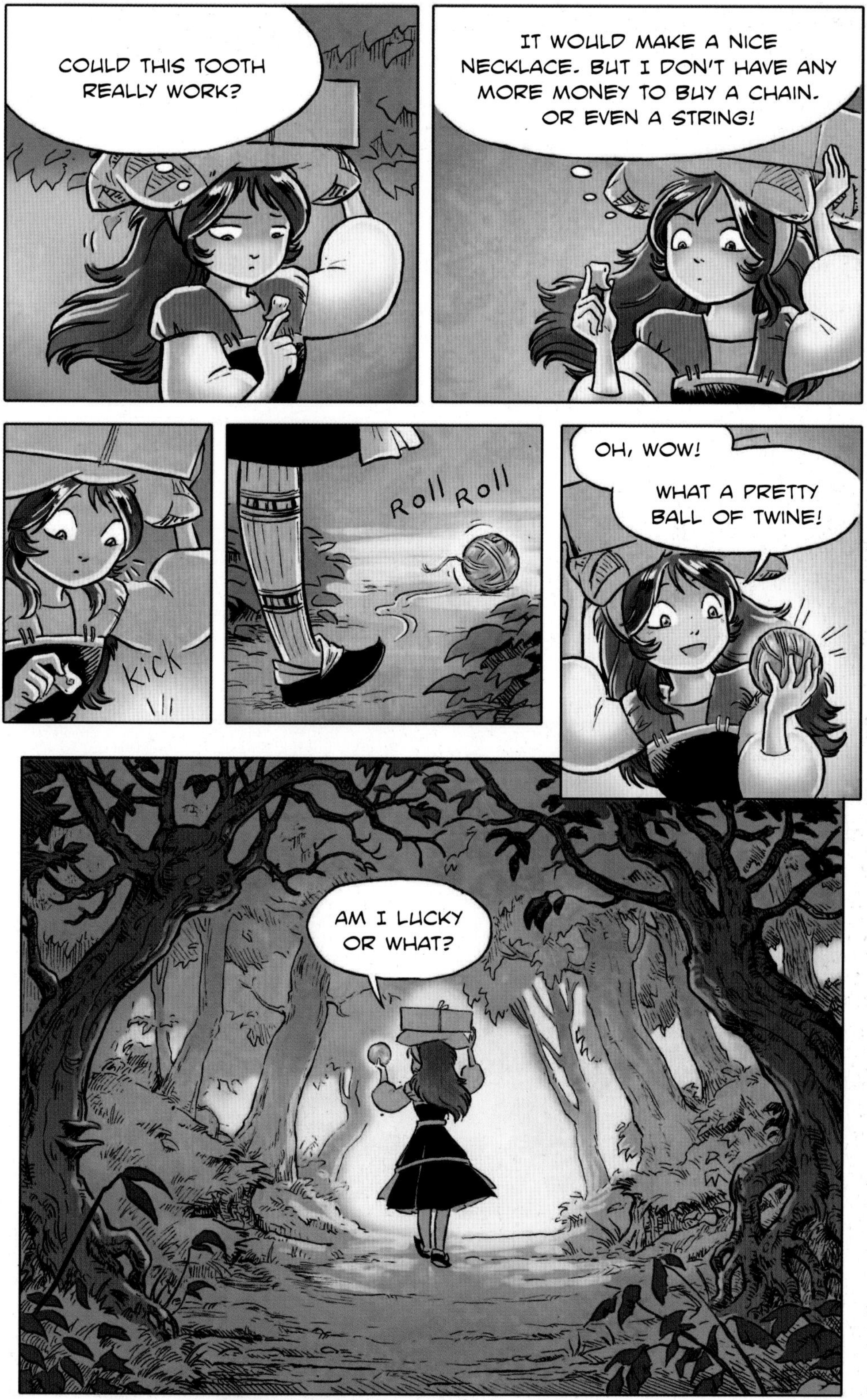
COULD THIS TOOTH REALLY WORK?
IT WOULD MAKE A NICE NECKLACE. BUT I DON'T HAVE ANY MORE MONEY TO BUY A CHAIN. OR EVEN A STRING!
KICK
Roll Roll
OH, WOW!
WHAT A PRETTY BALL OF TWINE!
AM I LUCKY OR WHAT?

45

46

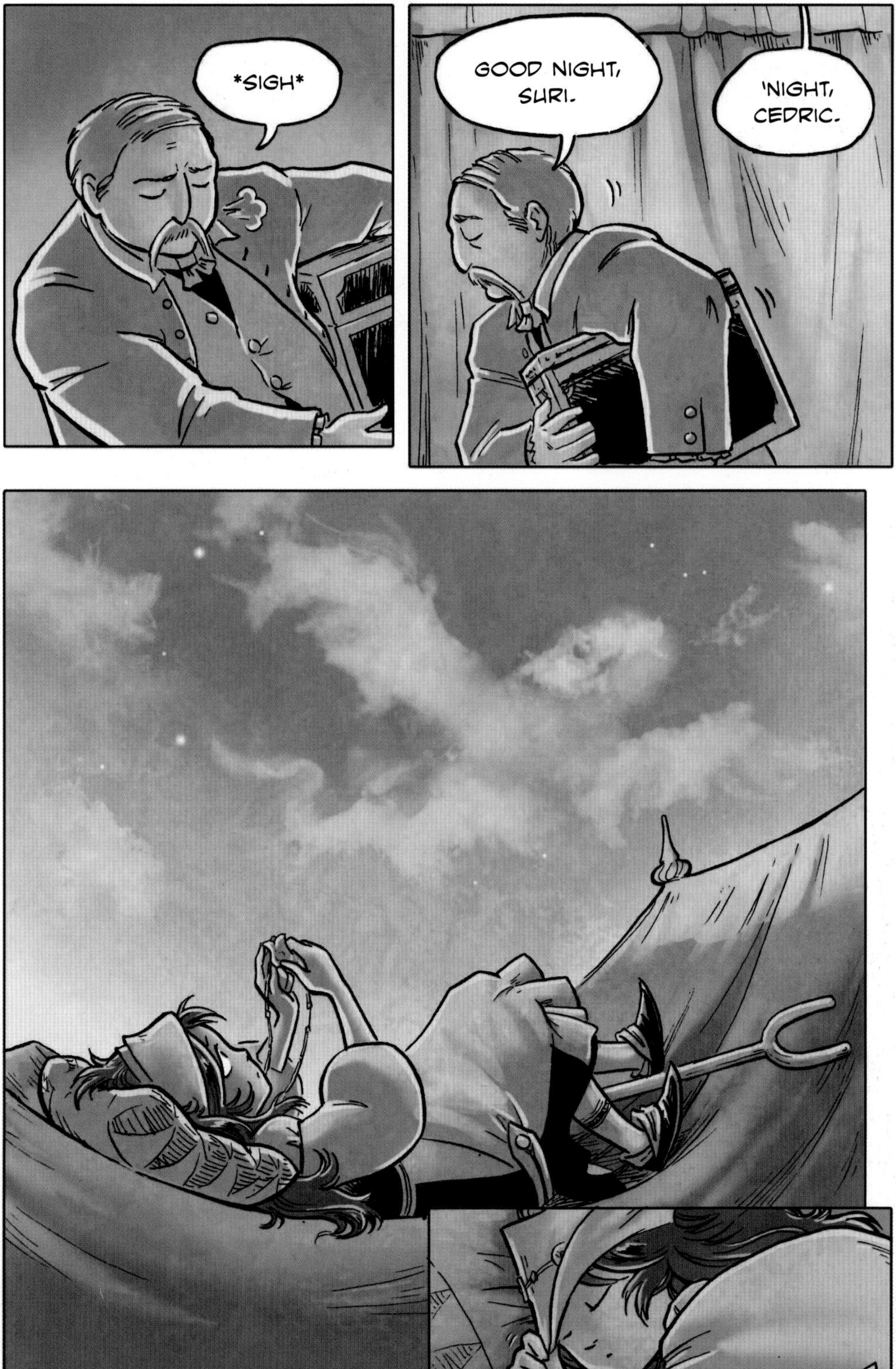
SIGH
GOOD NIGHT, SURI.
'NIGHT, CEDRIC.

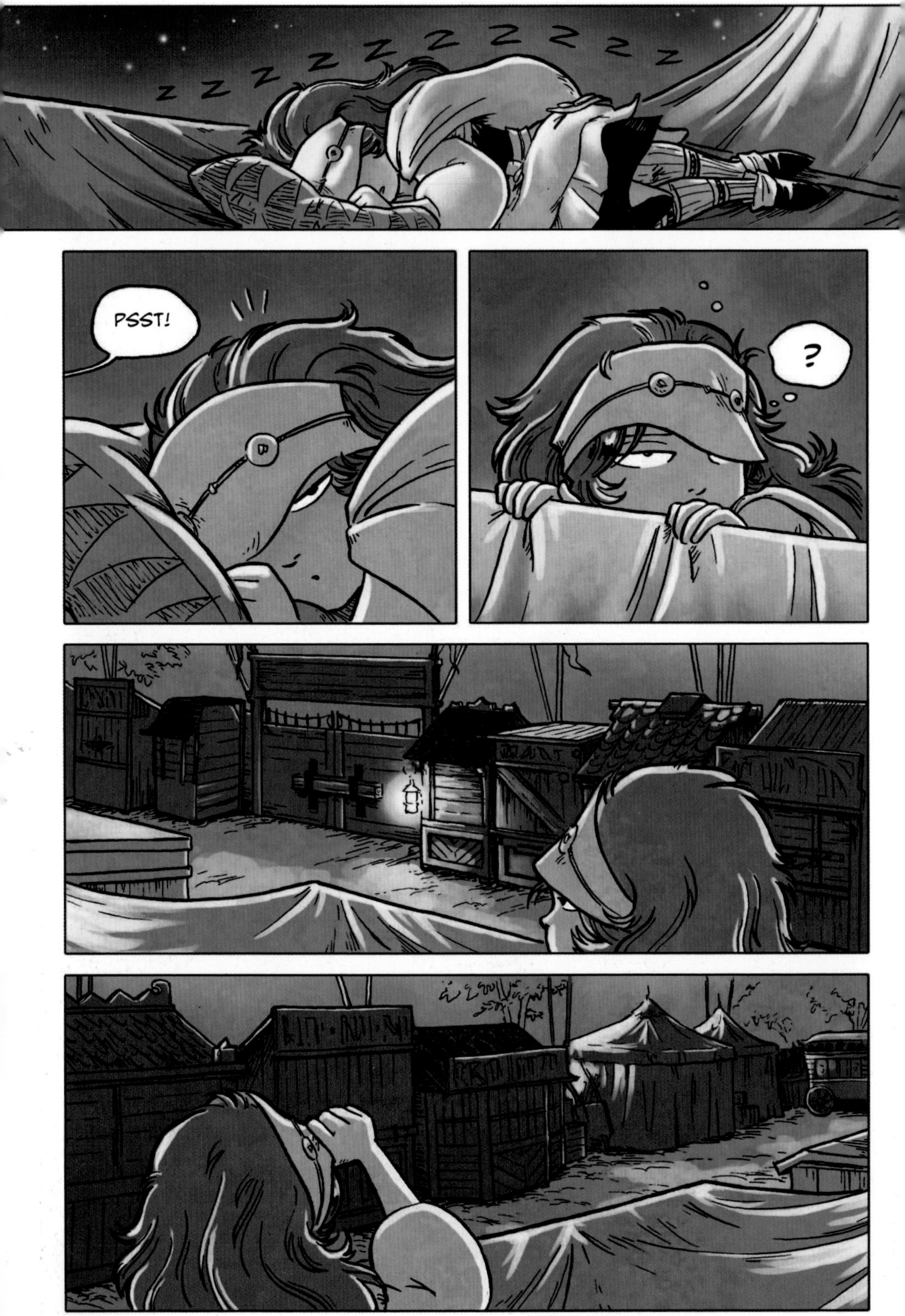
Z Z Z Z Z Z Z Z Z Z Z Z
PSST!
?

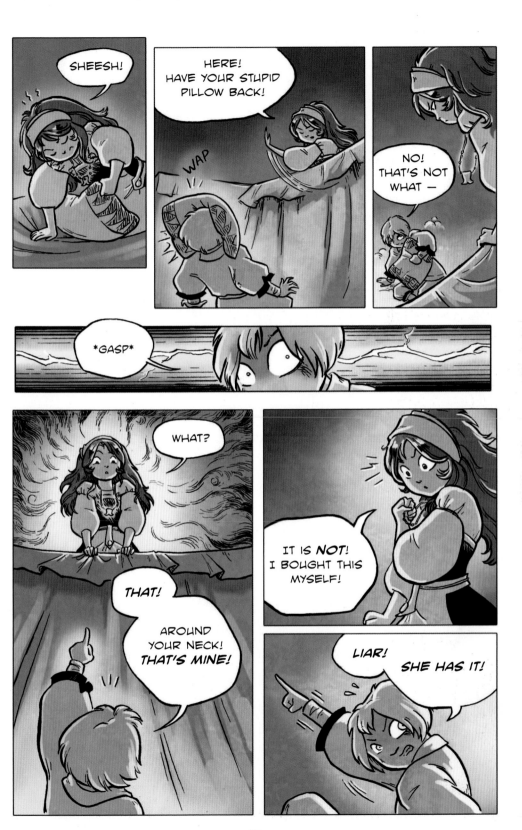

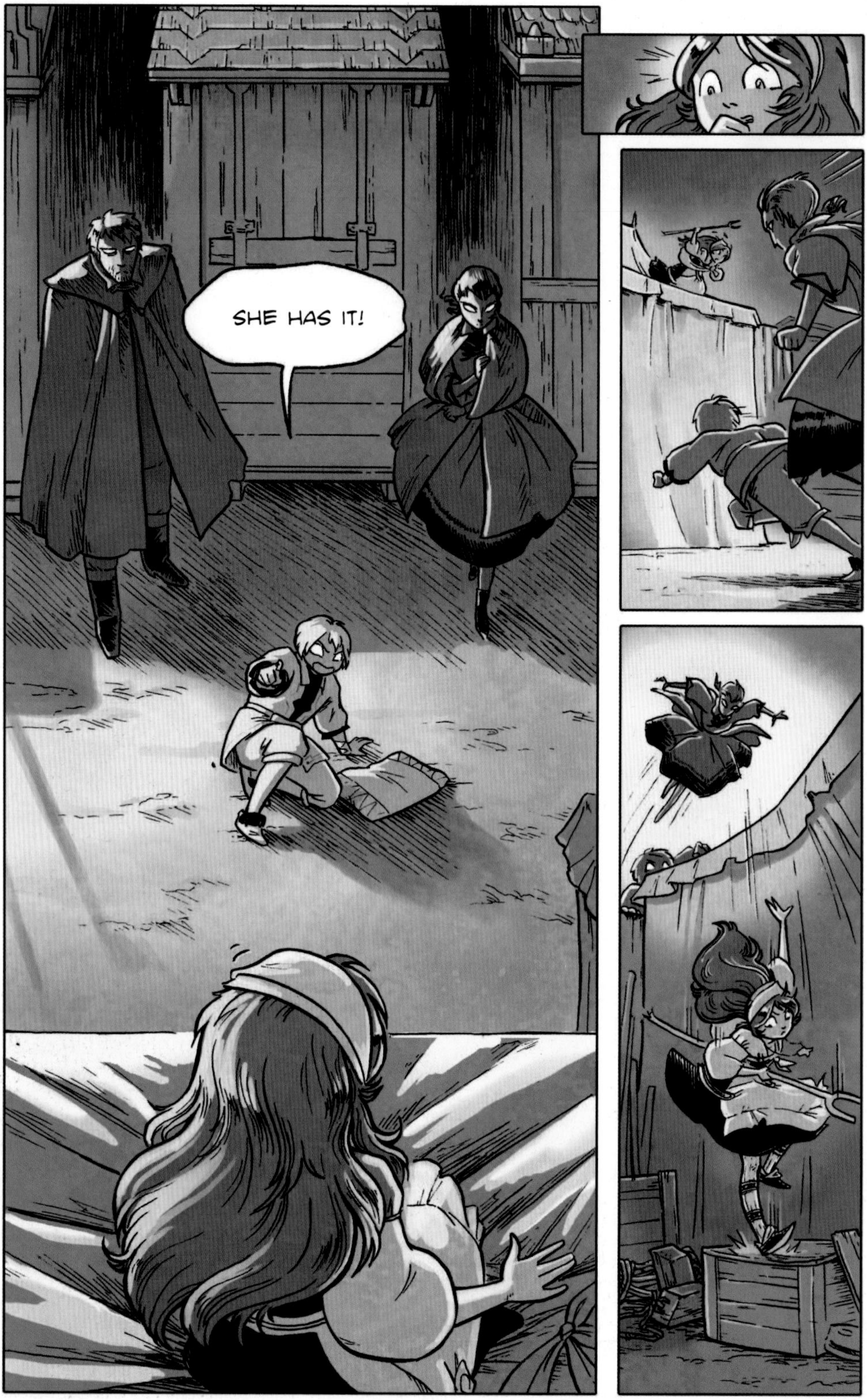
SHE HAS IT!

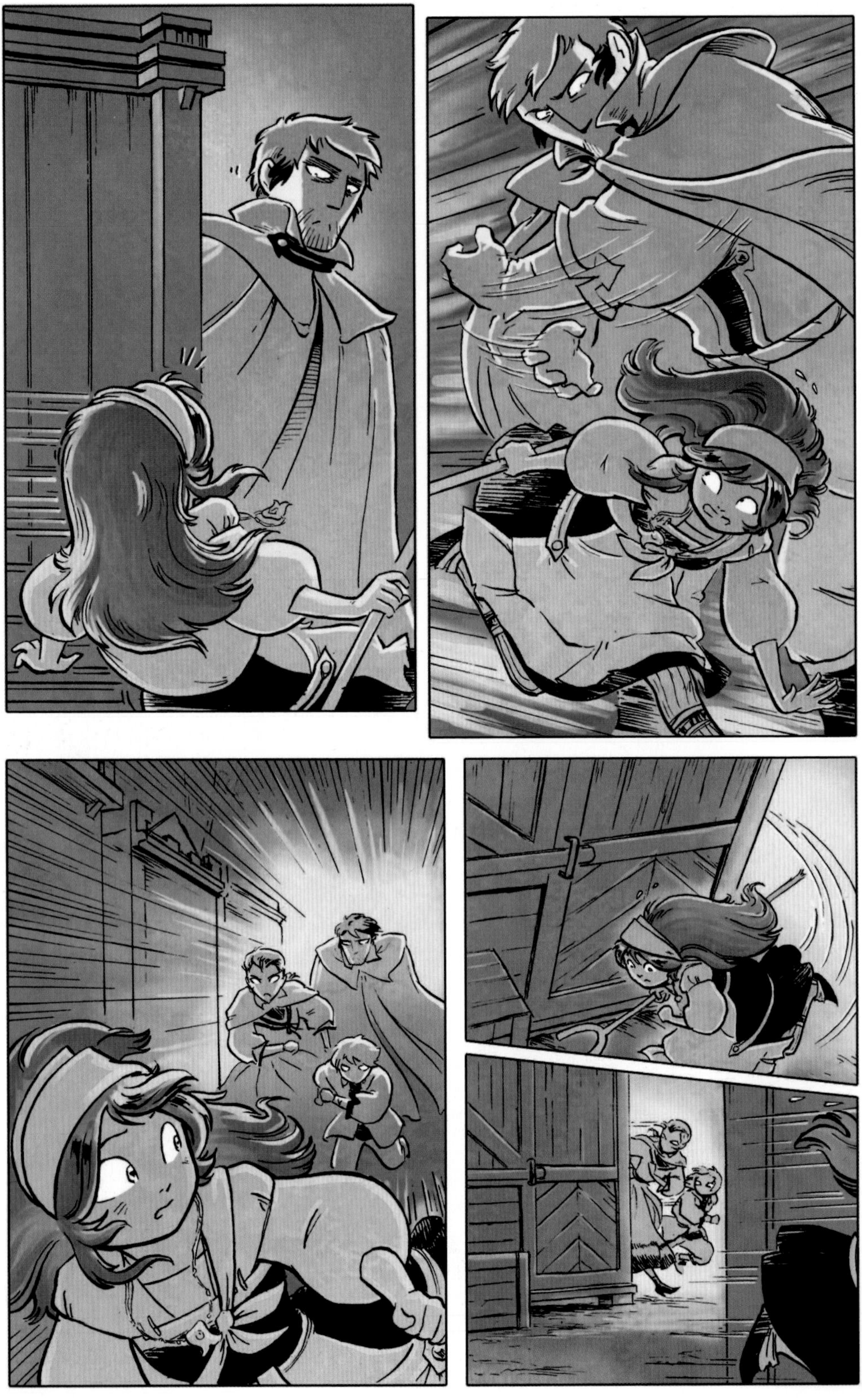

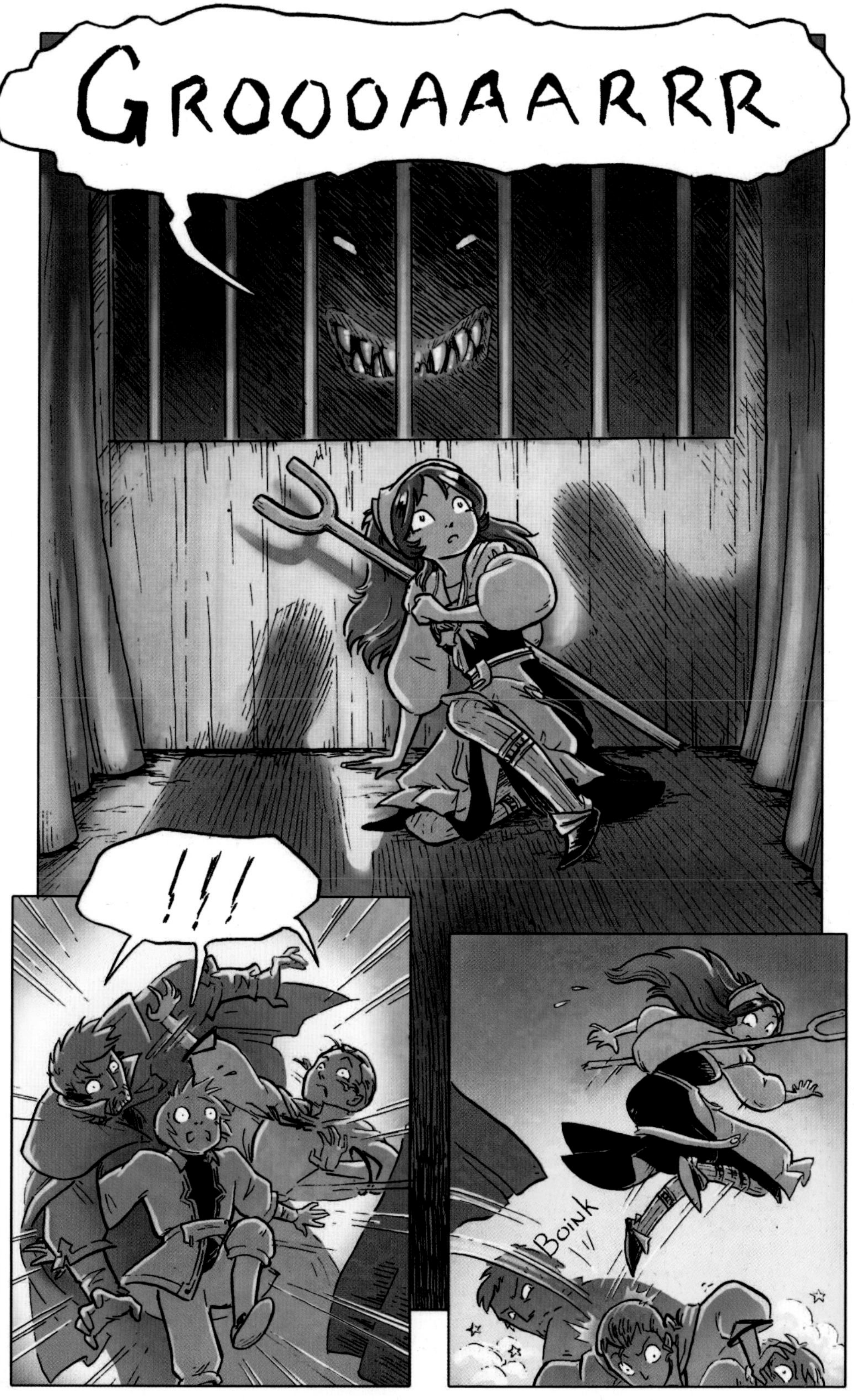
GROOOAAARRR
!!!
Boink

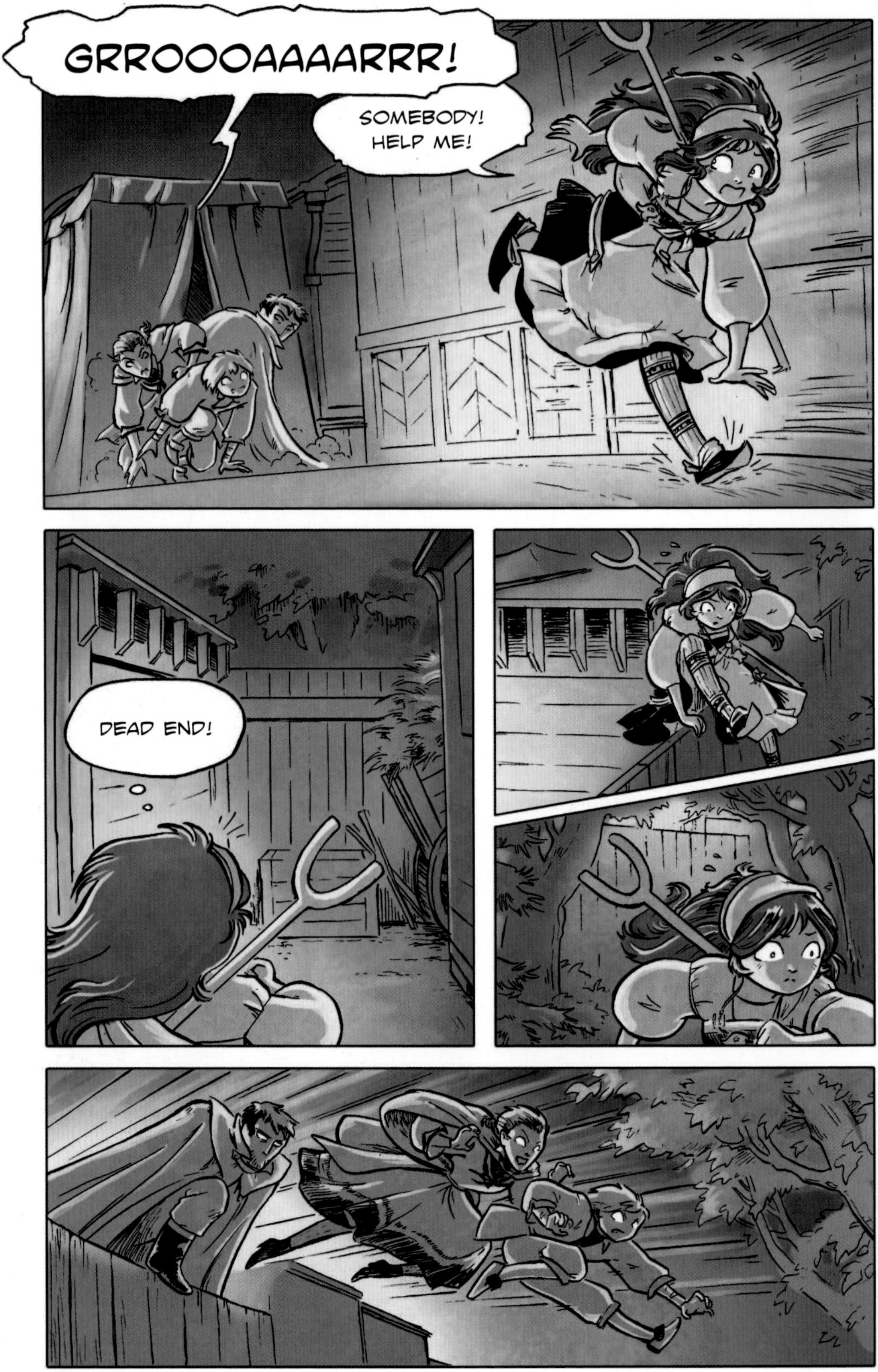
GRROOOAAAARRR!
SOMEBODY! HELP ME!
DEAD END!

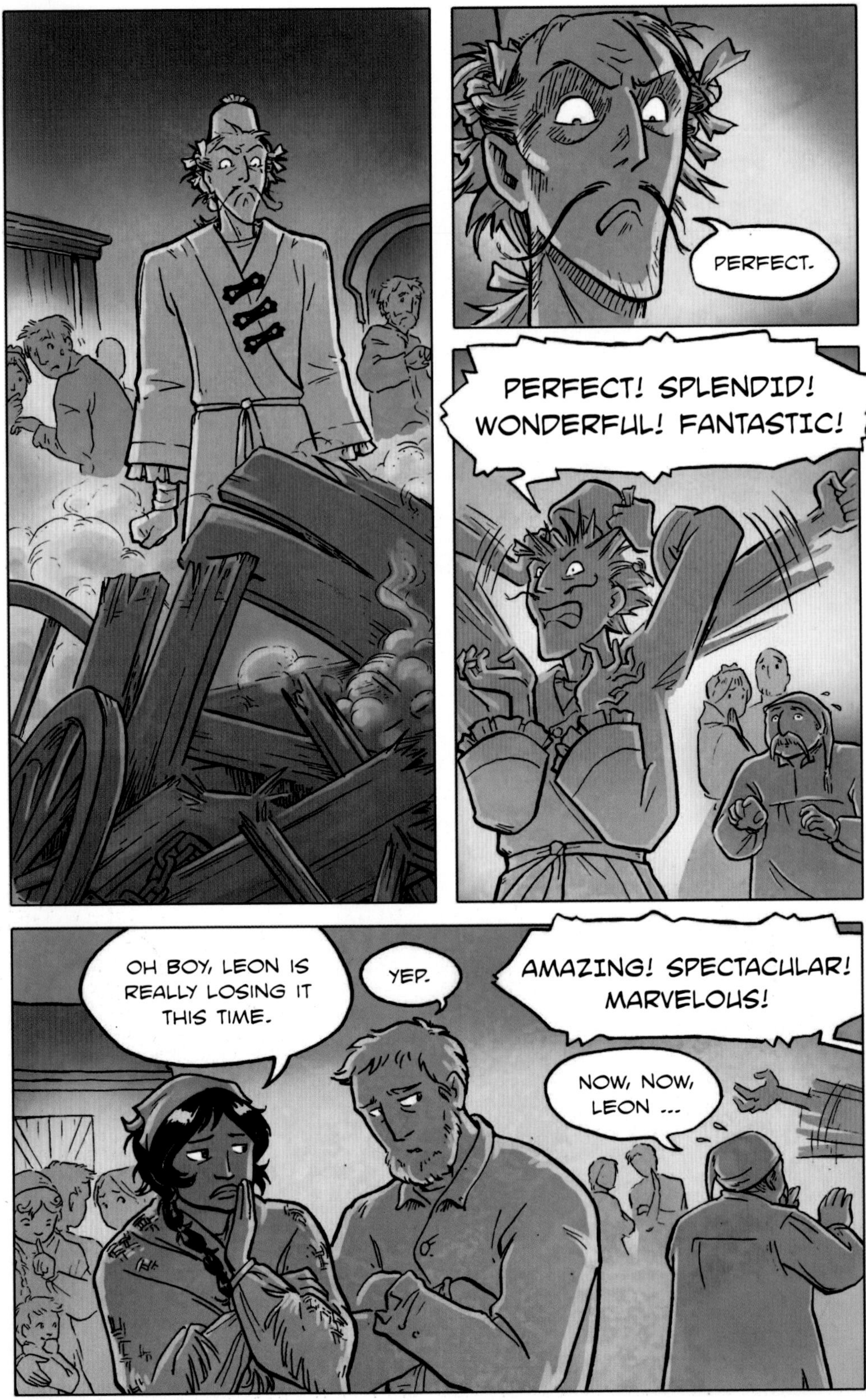
PERFECT.
PERFECT! SPLENDID! WONDERFUL! FANTASTIC!
OH BOY, LEON IS REALLY LOSING IT THIS TIME.
YEP.
AMAZING! SPECTACULAR! MARVELOUS!
NOW, NOW, LEON ...

HUFF HUFF

HUFF

FRTCH

FRTCH

I CAN'T RUN MUCH LONGER! PRETTY SOON I'LL HAVE TO —

— STOP.

70

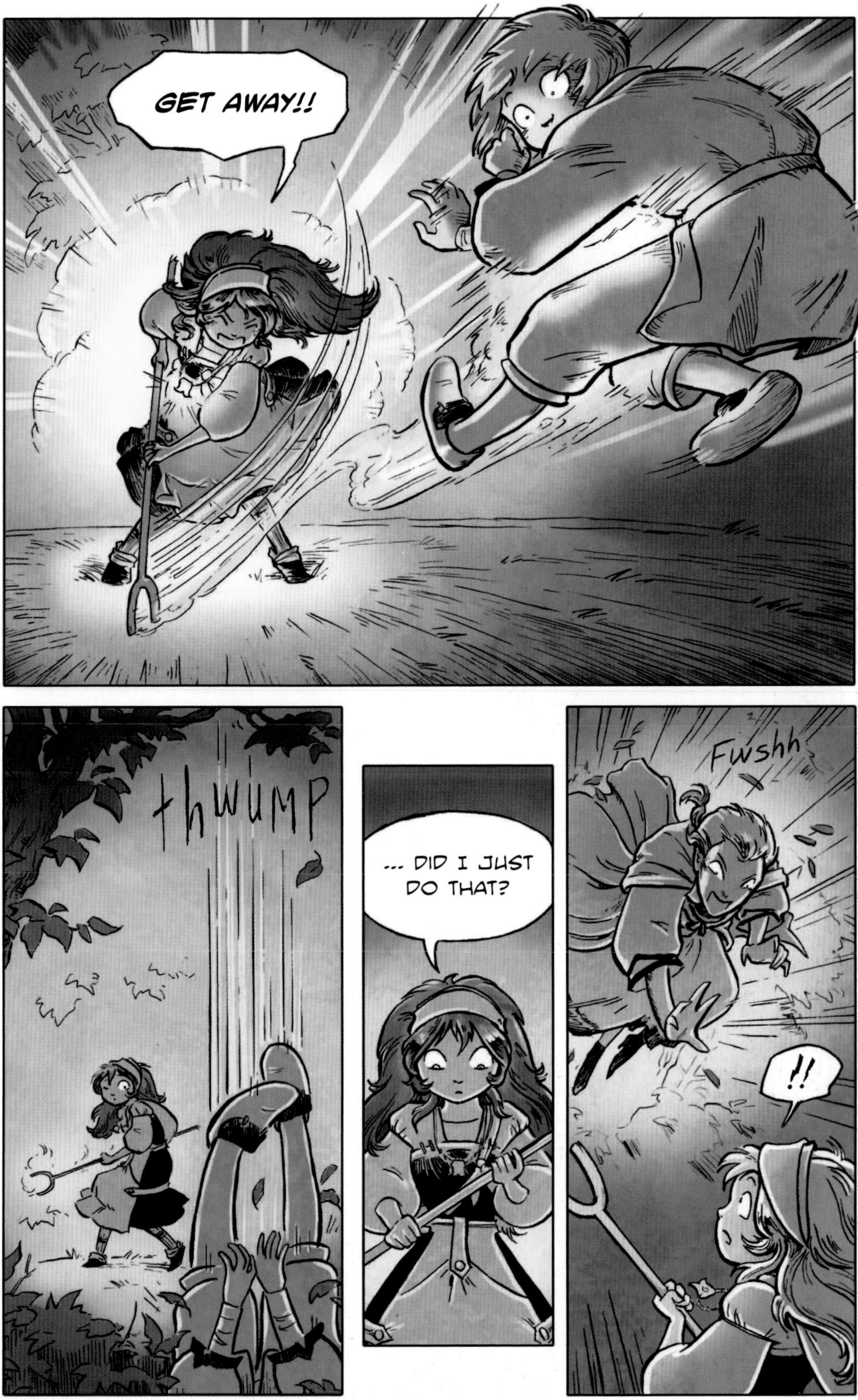
GET AWAY!!
thwump
... DID I JUST DO THAT?
Fwshh
!!

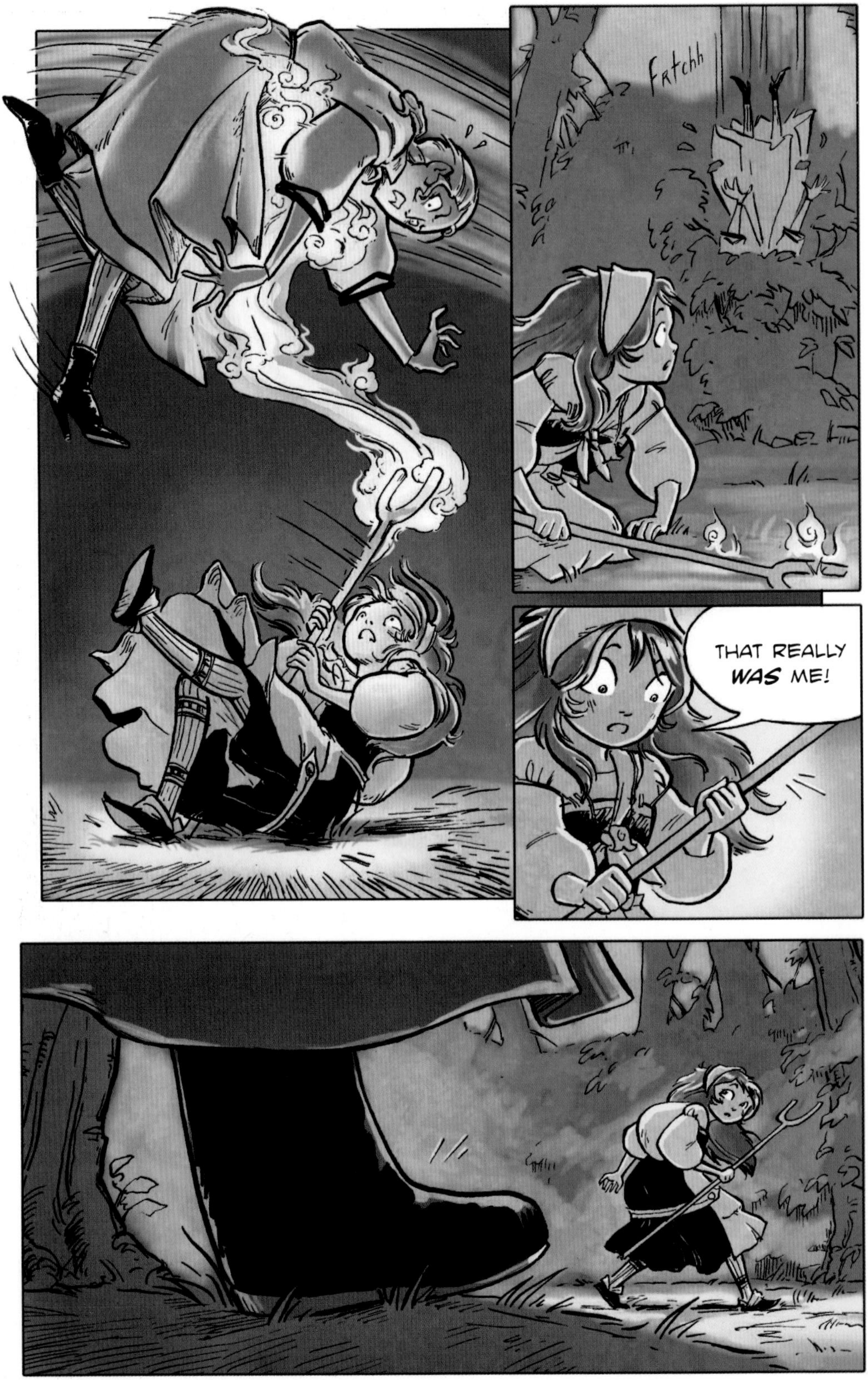
Frtchh
THAT REALLY *WAS* ME!

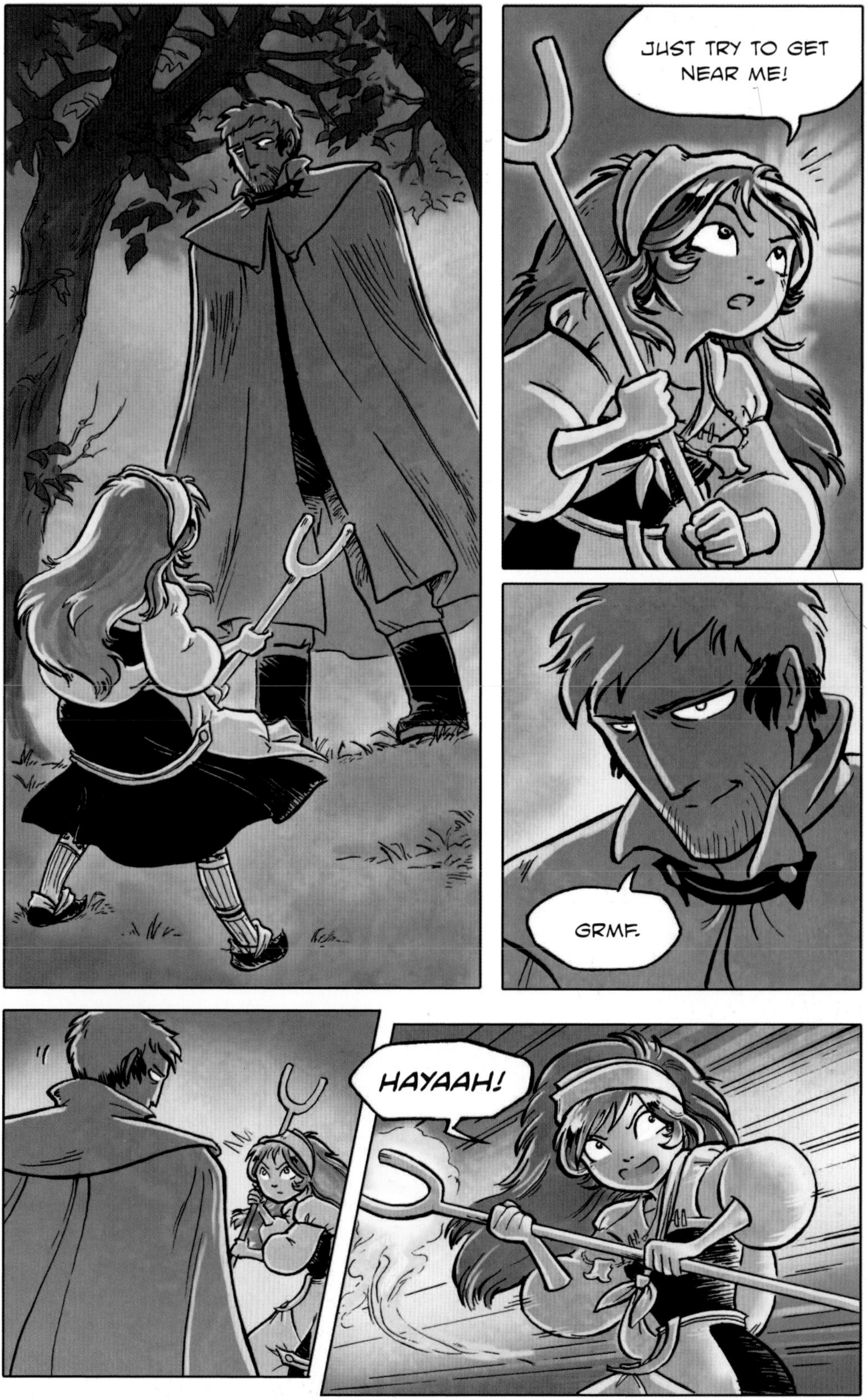
JUST TRY TO GET NEAR ME!
GRMF.
HAYAAH!

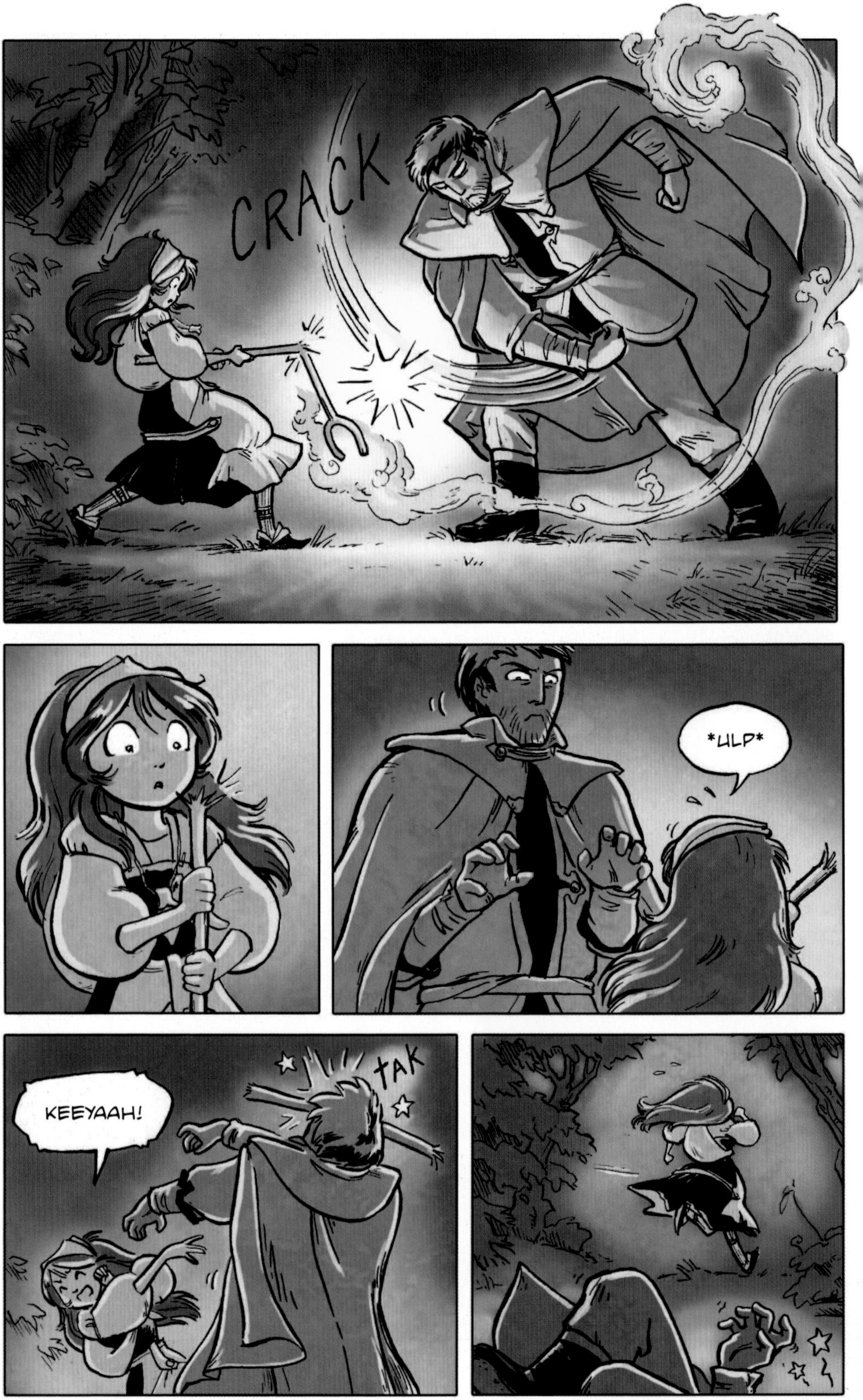
CRACK
ULP
KEEYAAH!
TAK

76

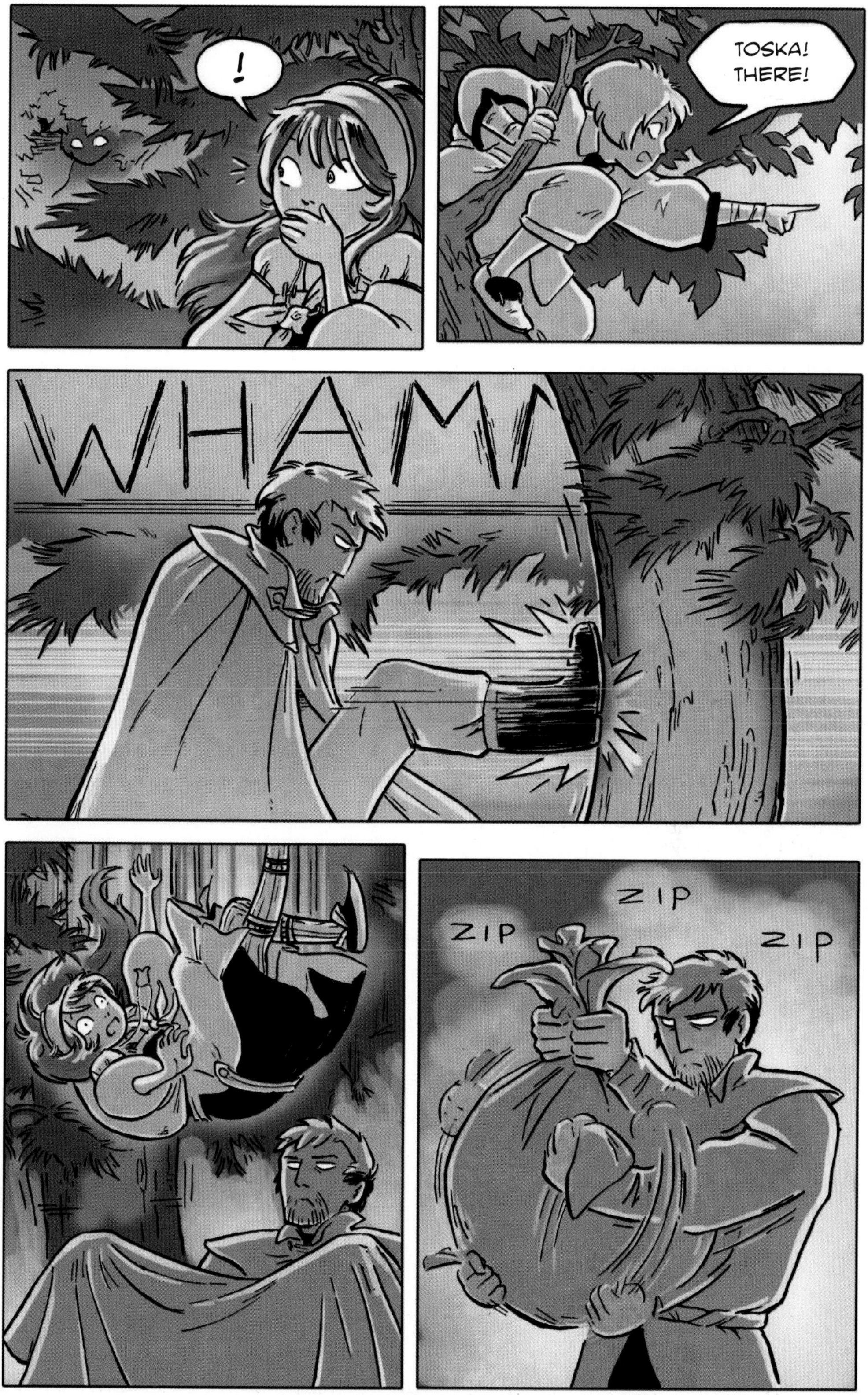
!
TOSKA! THERE!
WHAM
ZIP
ZIP
ZIP

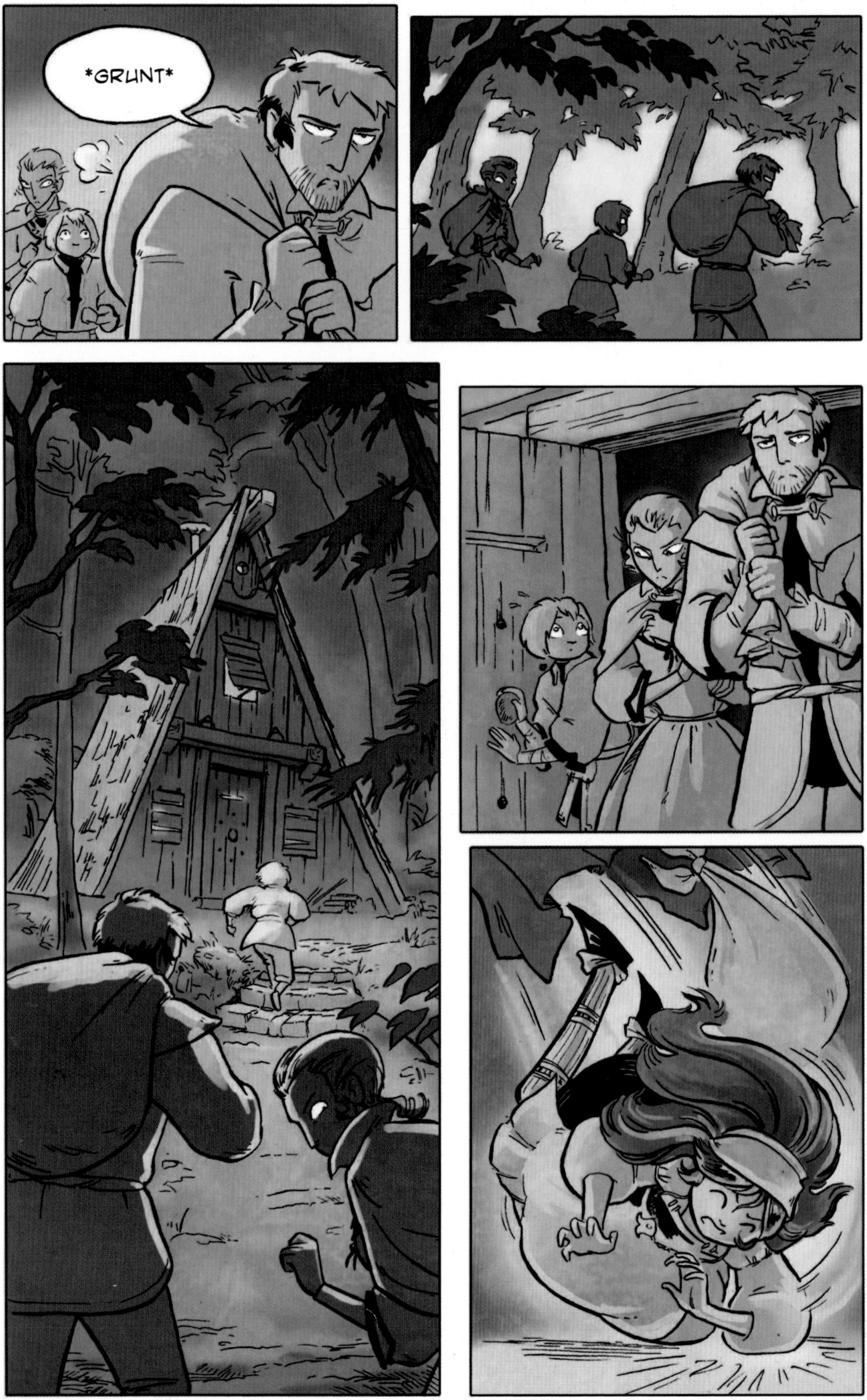
GRUNT

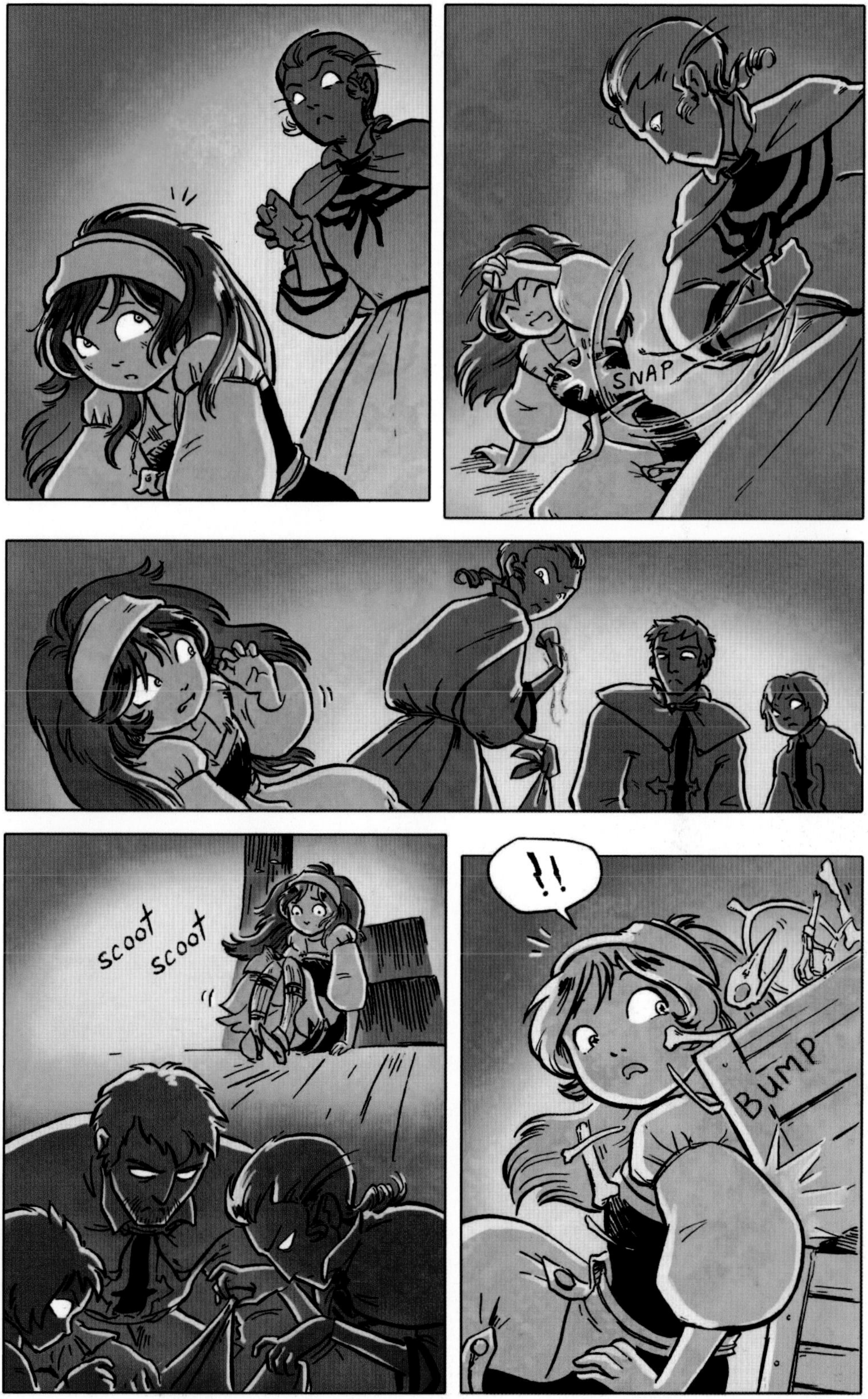
SNAP
scoot
scoot
!!
BUMP

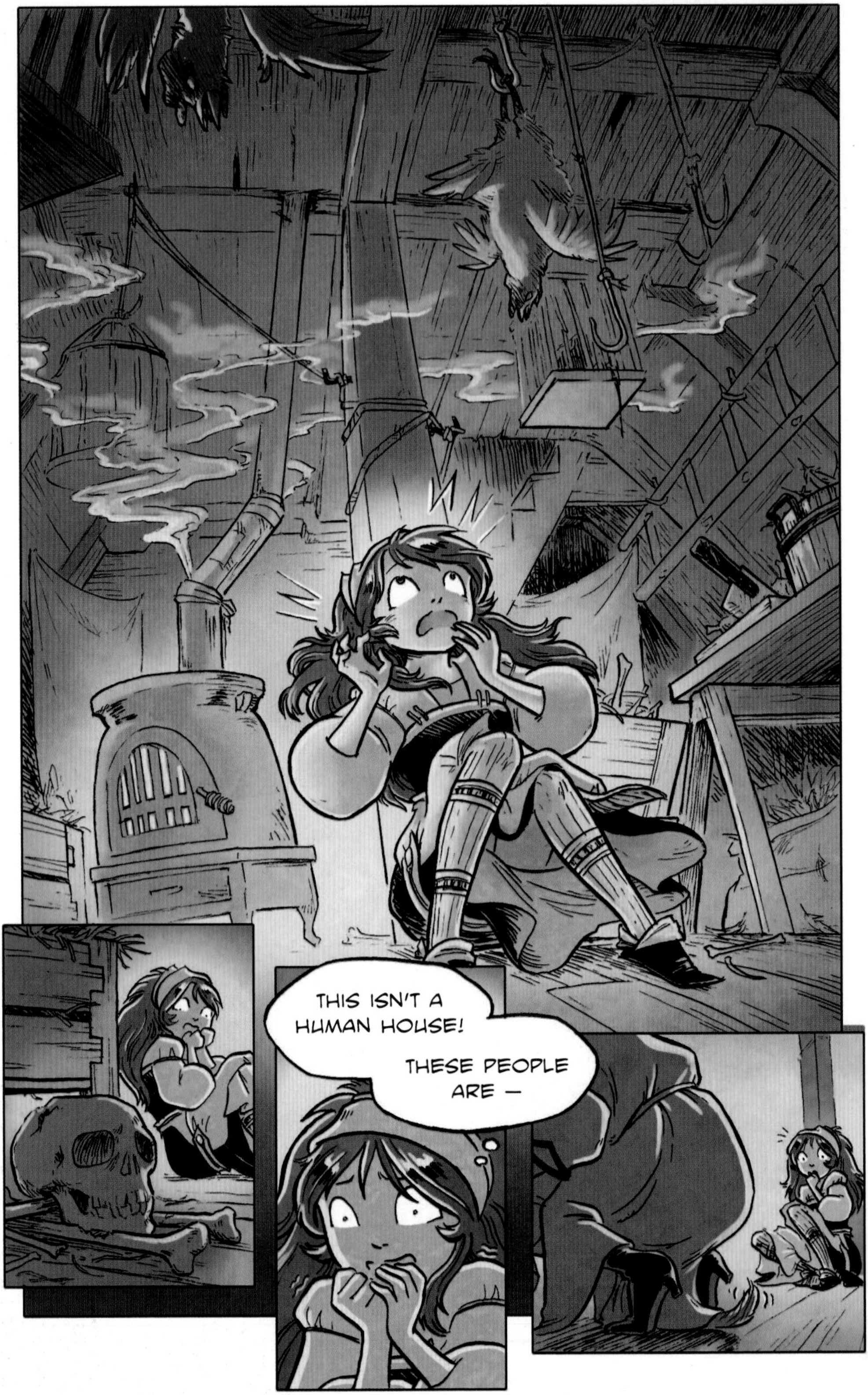
THIS ISN'T A HUMAN HOUSE!
THESE PEOPLE ARE –

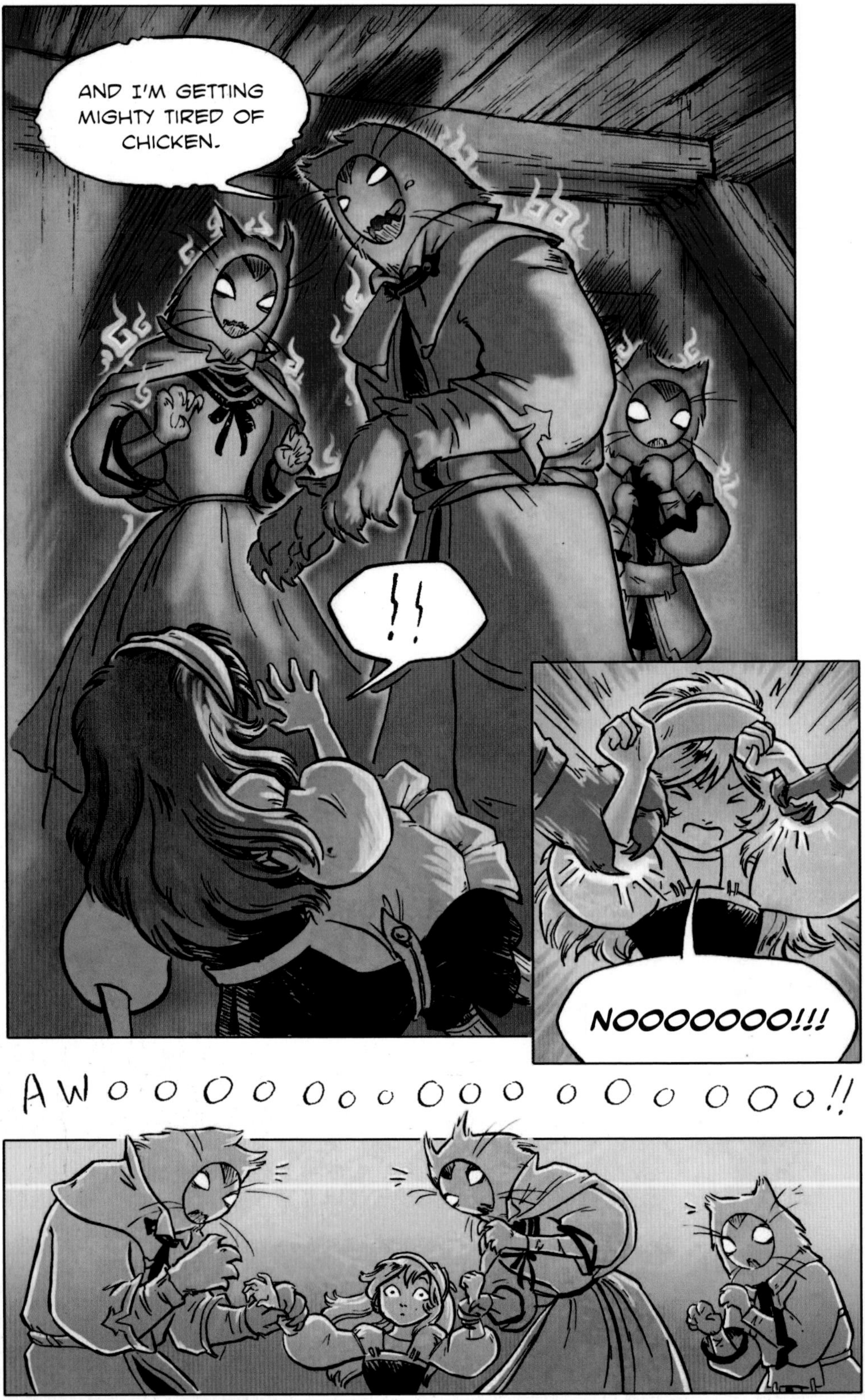
AND I'M GETTING MIGHTY TIRED OF CHICKEN.
!!
NOOOOOOO!!!
AWOOOOOOOOOOOOOOOOO!!

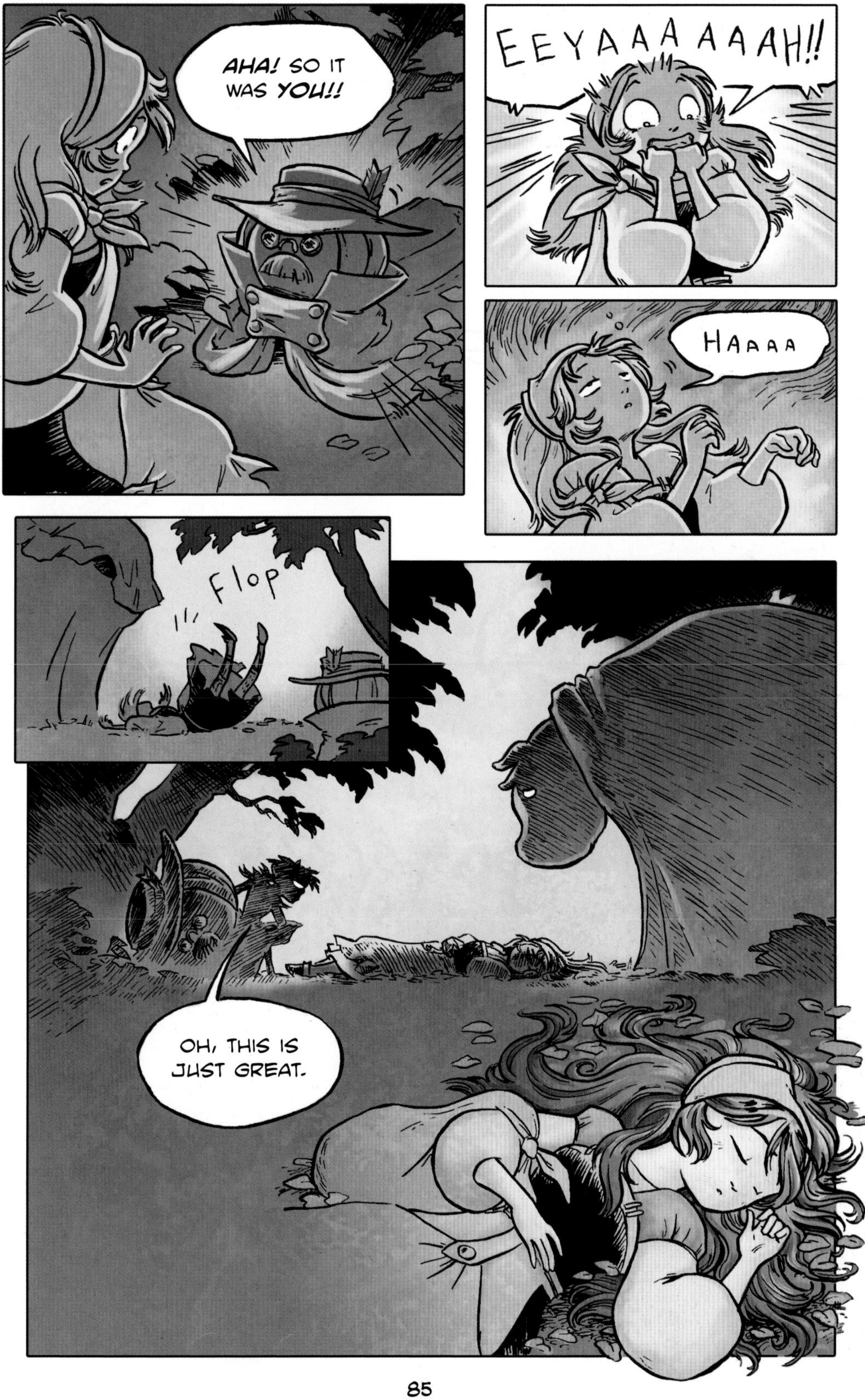
AHA! SO IT WAS YOU!!
EEYAAAAAAH!!
HAAAA
Flop
OH, THIS IS JUST GREAT.

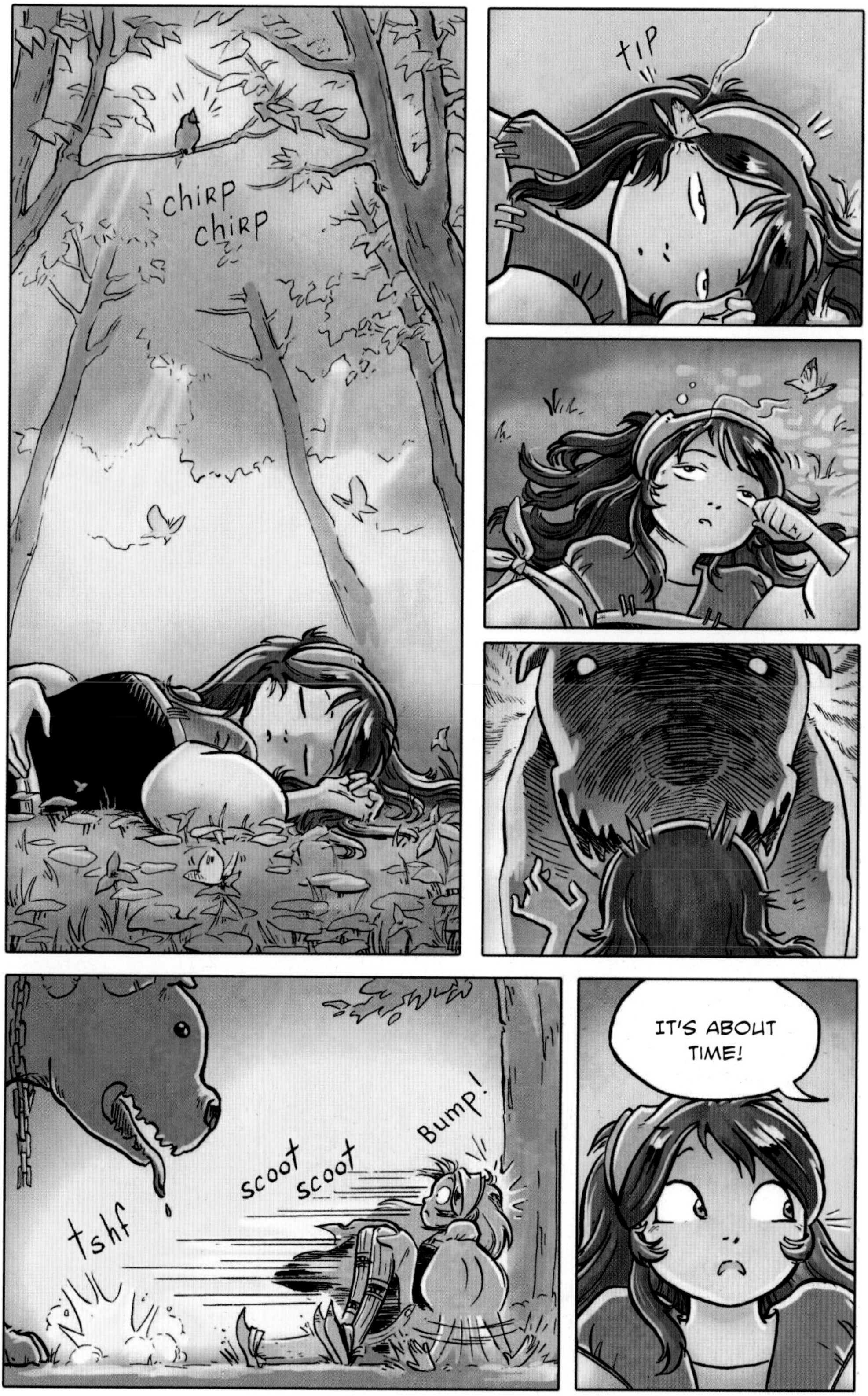
chirp
chirp
tip
tshf
scoot
scoot
Bump!
IT'S ABOUT TIME!

95

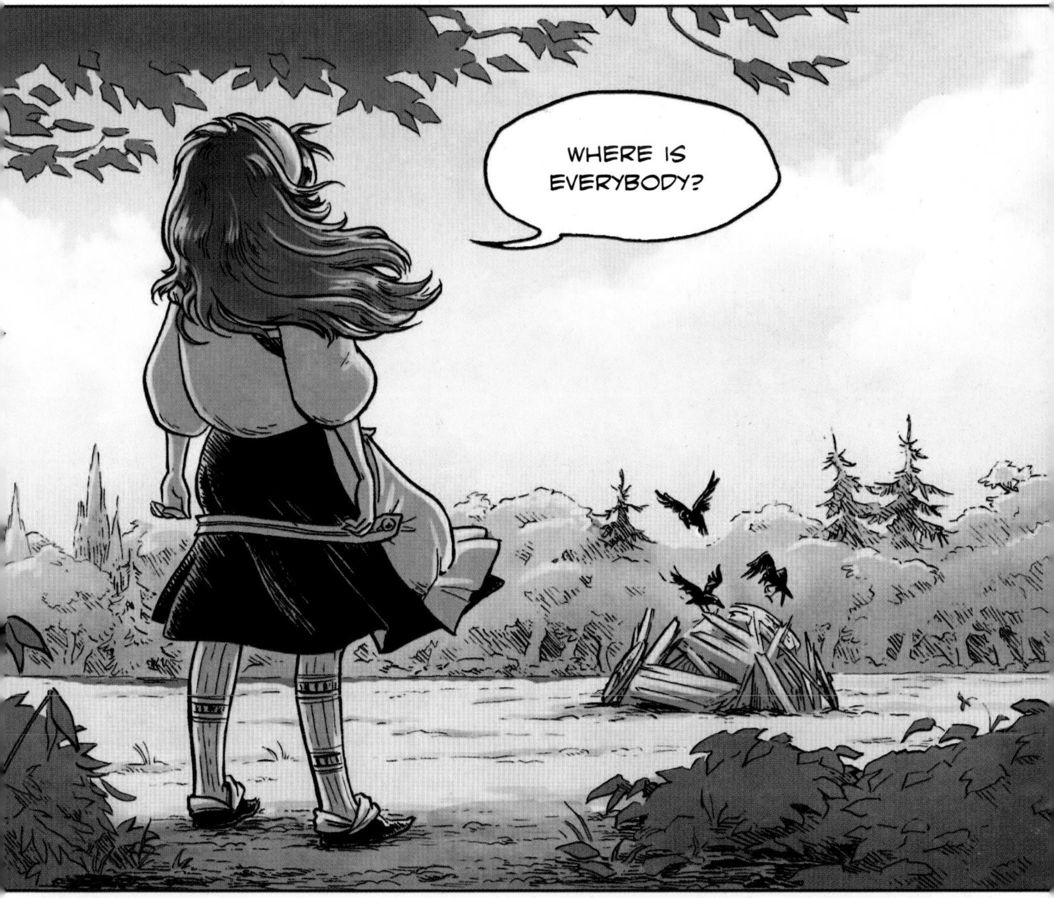
WHERE IS EVERYBODY?

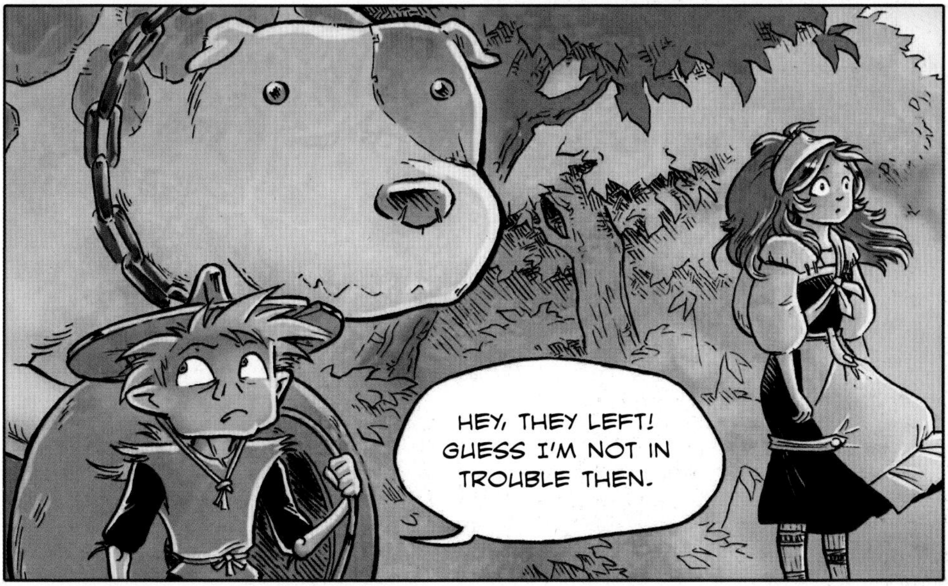
HEY, THEY LEFT! GUESS I'M NOT IN TROUBLE THEN.

98

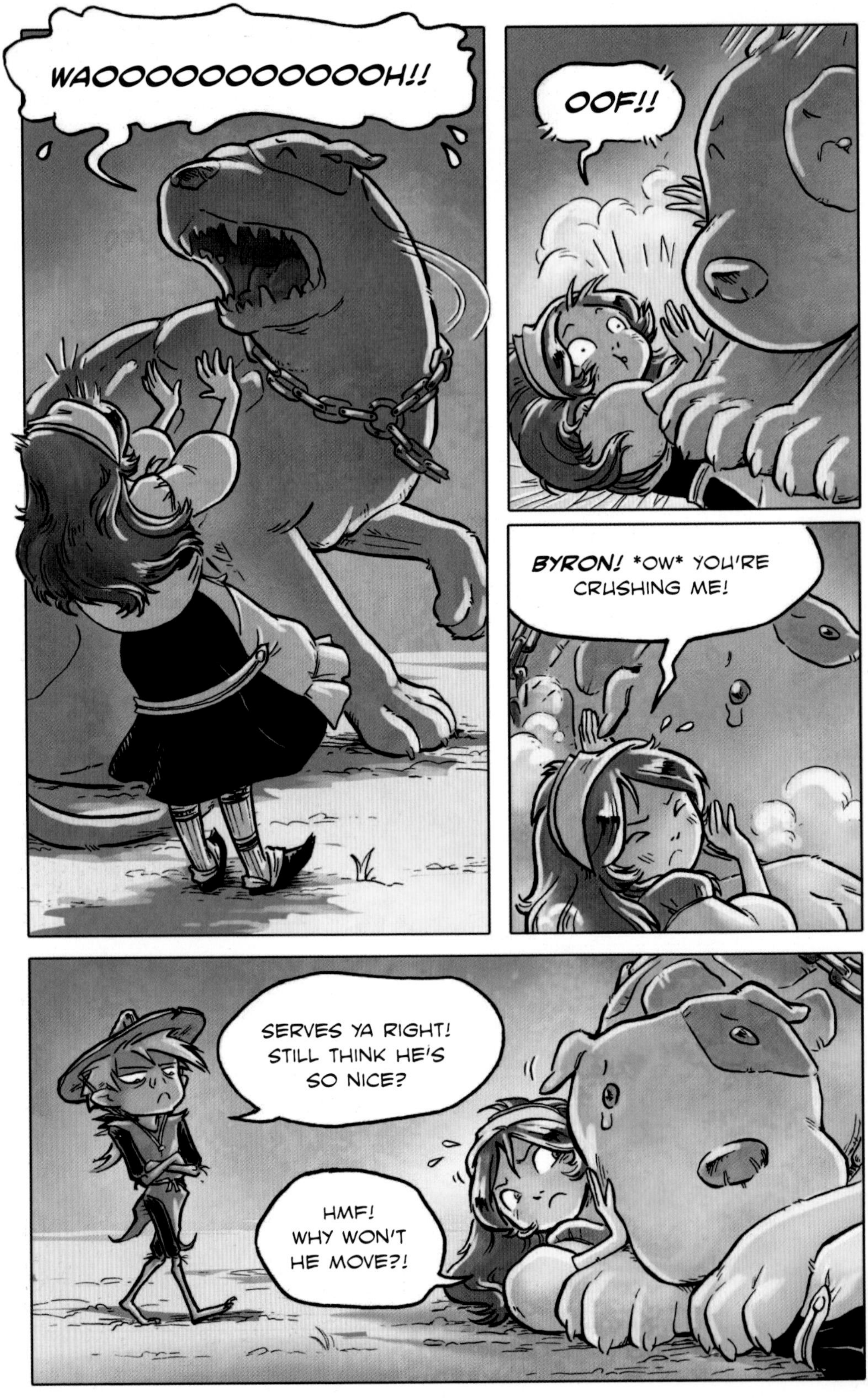
WAOOOOOOOOOOOOH!!
OOF!!
BYRON! *OW* YOU'RE CRUSHING ME!
SERVES YA RIGHT! STILL THINK HE'S SO NICE?
HMF! WHY WON'T HE MOVE?!

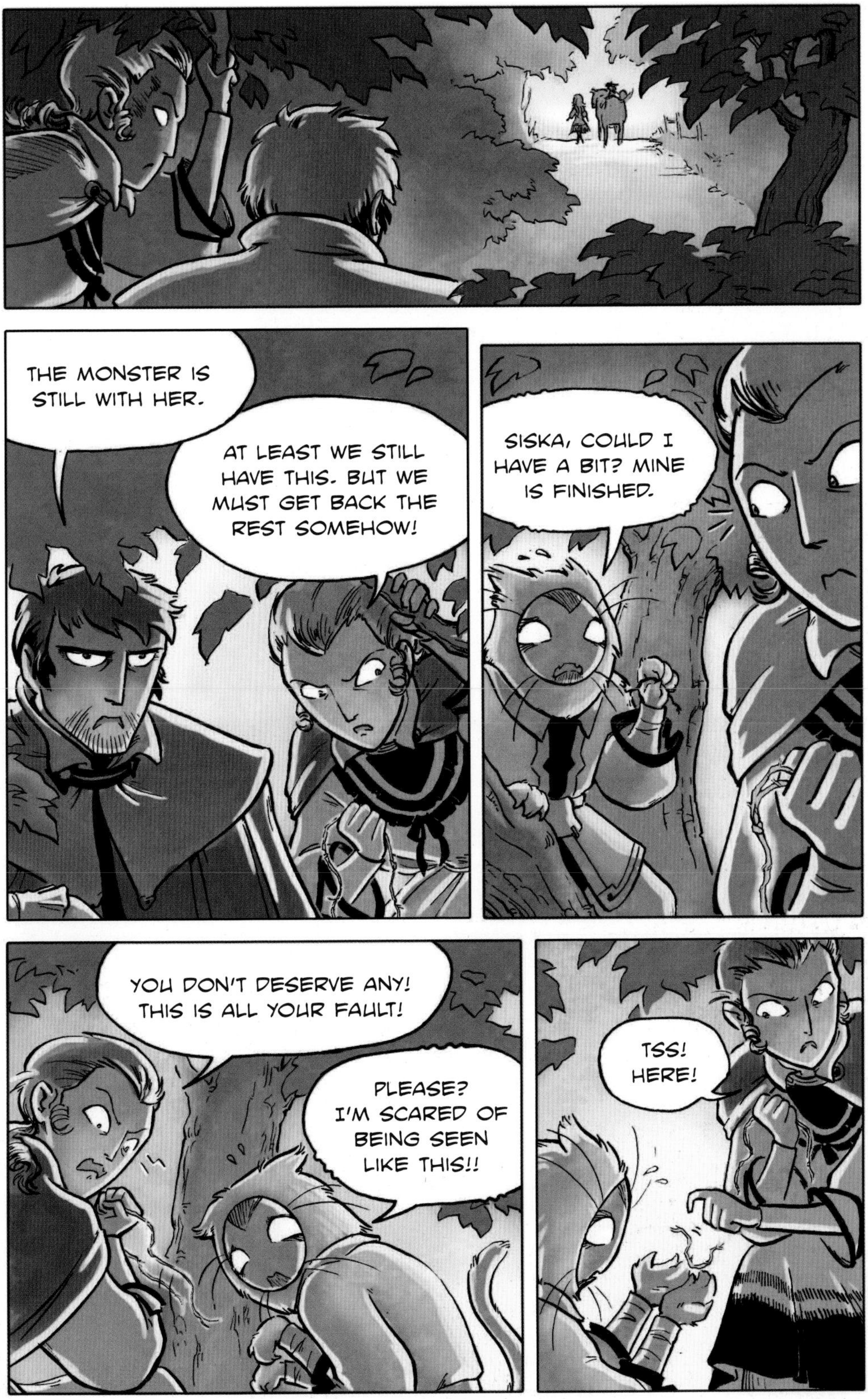
THE MONSTER IS STILL WITH HER.
AT LEAST WE STILL HAVE THIS. BUT WE MUST GET BACK THE REST SOMEHOW!
SISKA, COULD I HAVE A BIT? MINE IS FINISHED.
YOU DON'T DESERVE ANY! THIS IS ALL YOUR FAULT!
PLEASE? I'M SCARED OF BEING SEEN LIKE THIS!!
TSS! HERE!

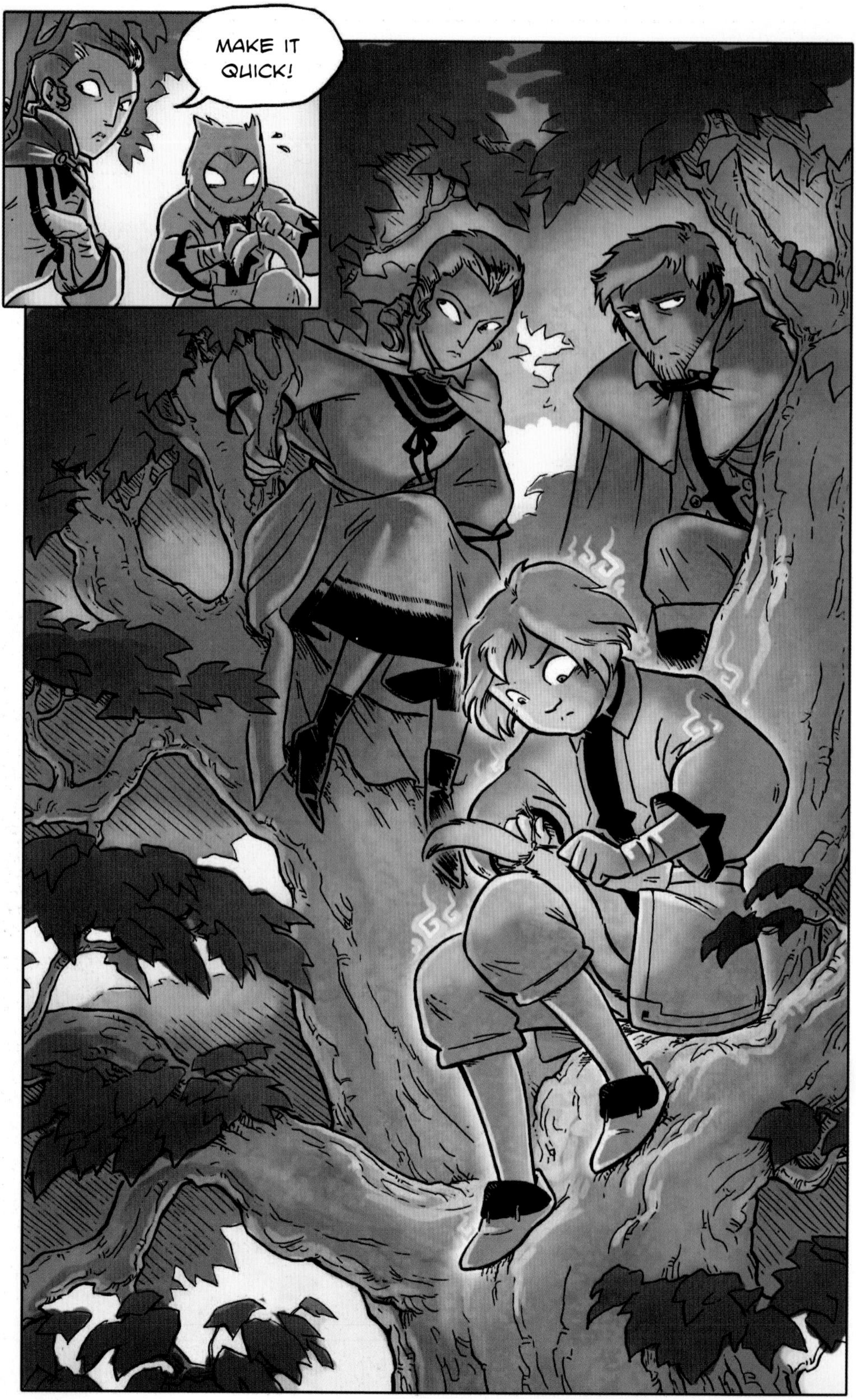
MAKE IT QUICK!

109

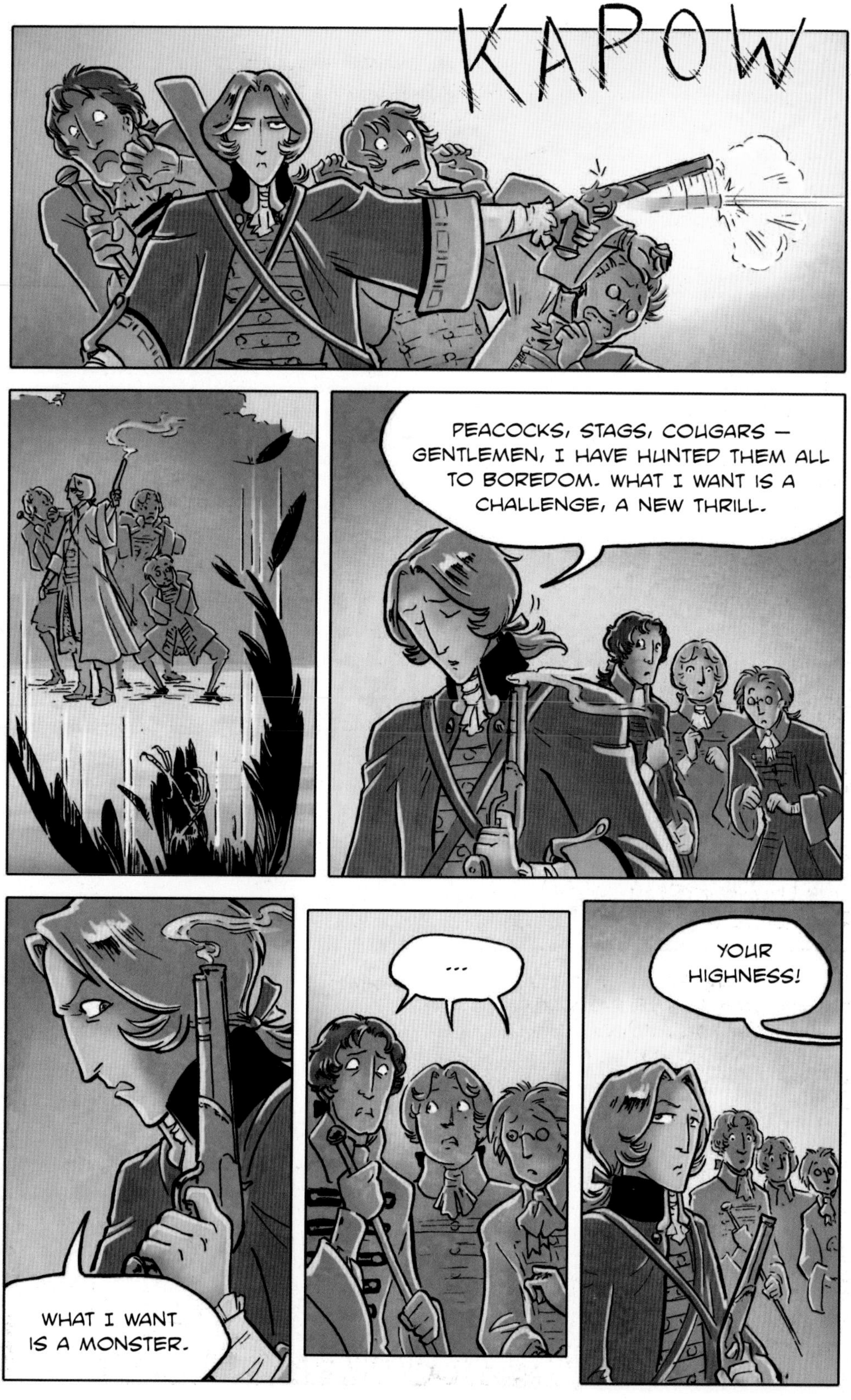
KAPOW
PEACOCKS, STAGS, COUGARS — GENTLEMEN, I HAVE HUNTED THEM ALL TO BOREDOM. WHAT I WANT IS A CHALLENGE, A NEW THRILL.
WHAT I WANT IS A MONSTER.
...
YOUR HIGHNESS!